Psssst!

The sudden hissing sound made Jason spin around.

There was something in front of the tunnel to his far right. He squinted against the glare of the walls. It was a long, low vehicle of some sort, and it pulsated with a low rumbling sound.

Suddenly a wing door opened on the driver's side. Out stepped a person — actually, *humanoid* was more like it. It wore a shining body suit with a bubble helmet. And in its right hand, pointed straight at Jason, was a gleaming metal gun!

Other Worlds of Power books
you will enjoy:

Castlevania II: Simon's Quest®
Metal Gear®
Ninja Gaiden®
Wizards & Warriors®

BLASTER MASTER®

A novel based on the best-selling game
by SUNSOFT®

Book created by F.X. Nine
Written by A.L. Singer
A Seth Godin Production

**This book is not authorized, sponsored, or endorsed
by Nintendo of America Inc.**

SCHOLASTIC INC.
New York Toronto London Auckland Sydney

Special thanks to: Greg Holch, Jean Feiwel, Dick Krinsley, Dona Smith, Amy Berkower, Sheila Callahan, Nancy Smith, Joan Giurdanella, and especially Bob Bernstein and Karen Janusz.

ISBN 0-590-43778-X

12 11 10 9 8 7 6 5 4 3 2   0 1 2 3/9

Printed in the U.S.A.   01

First Scholastic printing, July 1990

*This book is dedicated to Eric Leinwand —
a true Video Game Champion.*

CHAPTER 1

R-beeeak!

Jason Frudnick stood outside the black door. Gray, steamy clouds whirled around his feet. He felt as if he were floating.

R-beeeak!

There it was again. That sound was driving him crazy. Something was behind that door. All he had to do was reach out and turn the knob.

But a voice inside him said, "Run away. Run away or you'll be sorry."

Instead, he took a step forward. He couldn't stop himself. His fingertips stretched toward the knob, but he yanked them away. It was turn back now, or —

R-beeeak!

That did it. He couldn't stand it any longer. He had to find out what was making that noise. Lunging forward, he gripped the knob. It stuck to his hand, and a frozen slime oozed between his fingers.

He turned it. In the night's stillness, the click of the latch sounded like a gunshot.

1

With a deafening *creeeeeak,* the door opened.

Inside the room, it was black. Inky black. The black of the deepest spot in the universe, beyond stars, beyond light. Cold fear shot through Jason. His blood turned to ice.

He peeled his hand off the knob. He wanted to turn and run, but his legs moved him into the room. The darkness swallowed him. He looked around. Nothing there. The noise must have been in his imagination. Okay, time to go —

R-beeeak!

Before he could move again, he saw it.

It appeared in a blinding flash of light. Jason shielded his eyes. He couldn't see its shape, but he could tell one thing. It was huge. The size of a house. The size of a tyrannosaur back from extinction. Jason felt like an ant, a crumb.

He knew he had to look at it. He had to see the . . . the *thing* that was about to destroy him. The light was forcing its way into his tightly shut eyes, and he opened them. Slowly, into tiny slits.

And what he saw made his jaw drop open in shock. He choked back a scream. It couldn't be! It was . . . no, he couldn't even *think* it!

It was . . .

CHAPTER 2

Thud.

Jason fell to the floor.

His bed wasn't that high, so it didn't hurt too much. Still, it was enough to wake him.

He pulled himself out of the tangle of sheets. "It was a dream," he said to himself. Only a *dream!* He felt his heart beating a mile a minute, and couldn't help but smile with relief. Thank goodness things like that never happened in real life!

R-beeeeeeeeeeeeeak!

Jason's breath caught in his throat. The sound was real! It was coming from the box where Fred lived.

Fred was Jason's pet frog.

But this didn't sound like Fred. Fred's "voice" sounded more like *ribit* most of the time. Sometimes, if he got excited, it was *ribeet*. But never —

R-beeeeeeeeeeeeeak!

"Fred?" Jason called out timidly.

The morning sun was filtering through his blinds, casting stripes of light on the floor. It shone through the huge glass box on the table across the room — the home he had made for Fred. In the angle of the sun rays, Fred's shadow was a dark mutant giant.

"Was that you, Fred?" Jason asked.

Before he could even finish the question, Fred began jumping.

R-beeeeeeeeeeeeeak!
R-beeeeeeeeeeeeeeak!
R-beeeeeeeeeeeeeeak!

He was frantic. He was trying to leap out. Jason couldn't believe his eyes.

"Fred, what's the matter? Is something wrong?"

Fred began flinging himself against the glass — away from Jason and toward the window.

"You . . . you want to go outside?" Jason asked.

Fred jumped up and down, continuing his strange shriek. It was as if he *understood* Jason.

Jason was flabbergasted. He knew Fred was smart, for a frog, but he had never shown signs of understanding English!

"Feed him, for goodness' sake, Jason!" came a groggy voice from down the hall.

It was Mr. Frudnick, Jason's father, trying to get his Saturday morning sleep.

"Okay, Dad!" Jason shouted.

But he knew Fred didn't want to be fed. This was a stronger need, a need that would destroy Fred if it wasn't fulfilled.

R-beeeeeeeeeeeeeak!

Things weren't going to be too terrific for Jason either, if he didn't stop Fred from making that noise.

And there was only one way to do that.

"Easy, pal," Jason said. "I'll take care of you." He reached down into the high glass walls. From the bottom, the rich smell of the soil and mossy plants wafted upward. Jason had always been proud of the home he'd built, and Fred had seemed to love it — until now.

Jason cupped his hands around the frog and lifted him out. As soon as he set him down on the table, Fred squirmed away from him and jumped across the room.

He landed on Jason's blue carpet and hopped out the half-open door.

"Hey, where are you going?" Jason called out.

But Fred was already down the hallway. Jason followed him downstairs. Fred hopped through the living room, right up to the front door.

R-beeeeeeeeeeeeeak!

Jason shivered. What was making Fred act like this? He felt as if he were in his dream again — as if something terrible would happen if he opened the door.

"What is out there, pal?" he said in a soft voice.

Fred began jumping again, hurling himself against the door. His little body made sharp thuds as it bounced back.

"Okay, okay! I'll let you out. I don't want you to hurt yourself!"

Jason opened the door. In one bound, Fred leapt over the entire porch. He landed on the front lawn, and in seconds he was in the street. Jason had to run at top speed to catch up — which wasn't easy in his slippers. All around them, the small town of Batrachia, New York, lay asleep. The lawns looked a little shaggy, and Jason knew that the mowers would be roaring in a few hours. It was a quiet, small town by the ocean, and Jason liked it best on the days when the wind blew from the south. Then you could smell gentle, salty breezes. But when it blew from the east, the air had a stale, gassy smell from the nearby swamp.

Jason always kept his distance from the swamp. Everyone did. It always seemed creepy and slimy, and some people claimed that parts of it glowed at night. It wasn't the kind of place you ever really thought of visiting.

But it was exactly where Fred was heading.

"Not there!" Jason called out. "Come back!"

Fred was way ahead, at the very end of Archer Street. There were no houses there, just a cyclone fence. Beyond it, as far as the eye could see, was the swamp.

By now, Fred was a hopping silhouette in the orange glow of the rising sun. Through squinted eyes, Jason looked on in horror as Fred wriggled his way under the fence. He disappeared into the tall swamp grass, appearing again only at the top of each hop.

Leaping over the fence, Jason landed in the swamp and started running. Actually, slogging was more like it. Before long his slippers were sucked into the muck. Barefooted, he followed Fred into an area of bushes and scrawny trees. He pushed aside the spindly branches that whipped against his face.

It was no use. Fred had vanished into the bushes. There would be no way to find him now.

"Fred!" Jason was screaming now. This couldn't be happening. Not to Fred, his best friend! Not to the pet Jason had raised from a tadpole! Fred couldn't *possibly* survive in a swamp.

"Fred! Where are you?"

Jason's answer came—but it wasn't a frog sound. It was a low, sinister hum to his left. Jason pushed aside some thick, overgrown vines and followed the noise.

He came to another field. The grass here was pale, almost brown. It looked as if it had been scorched in the sun.

There was a dull, sickly green glow in the middle of it. Jason cautiously approached. Soon he could see where the glow came from—a strange metallic box that jutted out of the ground. On top of it was a small shadow that seemed to be growing. It was in the shape of a — frog.

"There you are!" Jason shouted. "I thought I'd lost —"

Jason cut himself off. He was sure he could recognize his pet anywhere, and this had to be Fred. But the size was wrong. Fred wasn't nearly that big.

Maybe it was a trick of the rising sun, a reaction to the swamp gas. Jason rubbed his eyes.

When he opened them, Fred was the size of a cocker spaniel. His little chest was puffing in and out furiously as he breathed. And with each breath he grew bigger. To the size of a wolf . . . a panther . . .

Jason backed away. He opened his mouth to scream, but no sound came out.

Slowly the box on which Fred was sitting began to sink. And as the top of his swollen frog head disappeared beneath the ground, Jason could swear he saw a look of fear and panic in his poor pet's eyes.

GAME HINT

Level 2 earns the crusher.
Level 3 earns the hover.
Level 4 earns the key for Level 5.
Level 5 earns the diving bell.
Level 6 lets you walk on walls.
Level 7 lets you drive on the ceiling.

CHAPTER 3

"No-o-o-o-o-o-o-o!"

Jason's desperate cry sliced through the morning air. The rising sun burned fiercely in his eyes. He raced into the field, stumbling blindly through the grass.

He had only taken a few frantic steps when he slipped. He stretched out his arms, but it wasn't enough. With a sudden *whump*, he fell face-first into the mud.

Springing to his feet, he brushed off his face enough so that he could see. Then he ran to the hole Fred had sunk into.

When he got there, he stopped short. It was much bigger — and deeper — than it had looked from a distance. A full-grown person could fit into the opening, easily.

He squatted by the edge and looked in. "Fred?" he called out.

"Fred ... Fred ... Fred ..." was his answer — the echo of his own voice.

Echo?

Jason stared into the hole, which was the darkest black he'd ever seen, like the black in his dream. How could there have been an echo? Dirt and mud would *absorb* sound, not bounce it back.

Unless there was something else down there besides dirt and mud.

Thoughts jumbled through Jason's mind. Should he call the police? No, they would just laugh. Should he get his parents? They would tell him to get another frog.

That left only one choice, and Jason knew it was crazy.

But crazy problems needed crazy solutions, so Jason decided to do it.

He jumped.

"Yeeeaaaghh!" The scream tore up from his lungs. He was falling ... falling ... picking up speed, as if he were in a race to the center of the earth. The darkness gulped him up, and he saw nothing below him.

Swwwwiiiish! Suddenly there was something underneath him, something like a slide in a playground. The cool, curved metal chute guided him on a sloping path downward.

At the end of the slide there was a shaft of dim light. He tumbled end over end, finally dropping through a hole. With a painful thump, he landed on a hard, cold floor.

As he stood up, his bare feet tingled with the cold. His breath came in small white puffs. A steady *drip, drip, drip* echoed off the polished granite walls. The glowing metal chest was nowhere to be seen, and neither was Fred. Jason looked up to see the walls disappear high into the darkness.

That was strange. The ceiling was pitch-black, but the room glowed with the same bizarre greenish color as the chest. The light seemed to be coming from within the walls themselves!

He turned around and saw tunnels leading in different directions. Fred must have gone into one of them, but which?

Psssst!

Jason's heart skipped a beat. The sudden hissing sound made him leap with fright. He spun around.

There was something in front of the tunnel to his far right. He squinted against the glare of the walls. It was long and low, and it pulsated with a low rumbling sound. A vehicle of some sort. Jason carefully walked closer.

Suddenly a wing door opened on the driver's side. Jason froze.

Out stepped a person — actually, *humanoid* was more like it. It wore a shining body suit with a bubble helmet. And in its right hand, pointed straight at Jason, was a gleaming metal gun!

CHAPTER 4

Jason's hands flew up over his head. "I — I come in peace!" he blurted.

The figure came closer, keeping a tight grip on the gun. "Who are you, and what are you doing here?" said a voice from inside the helmet.

It wasn't the kind of alien voice Jason had expected. For one thing, it was definitely human. For another, it was definitely female.

"M-my name is Jason F-Frudnick, and I came here to look for my pet frog. I saw him sink into this hole, and — "

"You realize this is no place for humans."

Jason nodded vigorously. "Yes, yes, I agree. I'll be happy to leave as soon as I find Fred — "

"*Fred*?" The figure cocked its head to one side. "You do not mean *frog*?"

"Fred is his *name*," Jason said.

The figure let out a high-pitched giggle. "You must forgive me. My mastery of your language is never yet complete."

"I noticed."

She lowered her gun. With her other hand, she reached into the vehicle and pulled out a body suit identical to hers. "Here. Put this on. It will protect you from the cold and the radiation."

Jason took the suit from her and began slipping it over his pajamas. "Radiation?"

"Yes. How do you think these walls are eliminated?"

Jason furrowed his brow. "Uh, I think you mean illuminated."

"I am apologized. Quickly, come into SOPHIA 3rd, my vehicle. You do not need your helmet inside."

"Just a second," Jason said. "I've told you who I was. Who are you?"

"My name is Yvtrkizj," she said. "The closest equivalent name on this planet would be Eve."

"On this *planet?*" Jason repeated. "Is this a joke?"

"I do not see what the yellow center of an egg has to do with this."

Jason scratched his head. "Oh, you mean a *yolk —* "

"Quickly," Eve interrupted. "There is no time for small talking."

She jumped in. Jason pulled open the passenger door and hopped in next to her.

Eve took off her helmet, revealing a cascade of long red hair and a freckled face. She looked like a typical American teenager.

Jason's head was brimming with questions. But before he could open his mouth, Eve looked at him sharply and said, "You must to wear your shoulder harness."

Obediently Jason reached for the strap. His eyes swept across a high-tech control panel in front of him. There were about a dozen levers and buttons on it, each with its own label: GUN, CRUSHER, HYPER, KEY, HOMING MISSILE, THUNDER BREAK, MULTI WARHEAD MISSILE, HOVER GAUGE, DIVE GAUGE, WALL CLIMBER, CEILING TRANSPORT.

"What are these things?" Jason asked.

"They are weapon controls," Eve responded. "Can you not read the labels?"

"Of course I — *weapons?* Hey, look, I'm just a normal kid from Long Island — "

"Prepare for acceleration!"

Eve thrust her gear shift downward, and SOPHIA 3rd took off. Not gradually, like a car, but with the force of a rocket.

"Yiiiiii — " Jason felt his cheeks pressing backward with G forces, baring his teeth. There was a sonic explosion as SOPHIA 3rd shot through the tunnel.

As the ship settled into a cruising speed, Jason felt normal again — and angry.

He glared at Eve. "Look, you've been ordering me around, expecting me to obey your every command. Now I want *you* to answer a few questions. Where is Fred? Where did you come from? Where are you taking me? And what kind of place —"

Jason was cut off by a sudden, bone-jarring jolt. His stomach flip-flopped as SOPHIA 3rd suddenly dipped downward, then back up. "What was —"

Another jolt wrenched the ship. It was accompanied by a resounding *boom!*

Eve slammed on the brakes, and SOPHIA 3rd screeched to an instantaneous stop.

Eve was silent, staring intently out the windshield. Jason tried to see what she was looking at. They were on a long, narrow cliff. In front of them were more cliffs, each one separated by a deep dropoff. On the second cliff, across the dropoff, there was a robot the height of a basketball hoop.

Looking at the drop-off, Jason breathed a sigh of relief. "There's no way he can step over that," Jason said. "Let's get out of here."

"Incorrect on both counts," Eve said.

Jason's eyes widened in horror as the robot leapt onto their cliff.

Boom! SOPHIA 3rd jolted again as the fearsome creature landed cleanly. He began clomping toward them.

Each powerful step made Jason's teeth chatter. "He's going to get us!" he screamed.

"Fire at him!" Eve yelled.

Jason stared at the control panel, bewildered. He flicked the lever marked MULTIWARHEAD MISSILE.

Nothing happened.

Boom! came the robot's step. It was about six feet away.

"Fire!" Eve demanded.

Jason pulled THUNDER BREAK. Again, nothing.

"I can't!" Jason looked at Eve, shaking with fear. "Our power is gone!"

"Brace yourself!" Eve shouted.

Before their eyes, the robot left the ground. When it came down, its heavy solid-metal boots were aimed straight at SOPHIA 3rd!

CHAPTER 5

Crrunnch! SOPHIA 3rd sank a few inches. Jason looked up to see two clear footprints embedded in the roof.

On Eve's dashboard there was a bright vertical gauge marked POWER SUPPLY. It had been lit all the way to the top, but now the gauge was lower.

Crrunnch! The ship sank again. So did the power gauge. The dents in the roof were almost touching Jason's head.

"Hang up!" Eve said.

Jason knew what she meant — *hang on!* He grabbed the hand rest.

With a roar of its engine, SOPHIA 3rd lurched backward. There was a bone-jarring thud as the robot landed on the ground. "He is a heavy one," Eve remarked.

"We'll mail him a diet book later," Jason said. "Now let's get out of here!"

The robot turned to face them. But instead of backing up, Eve drove forward.

"Wrong way!" Jason shouted. "Put it in reverse!"

He closed his eyes and braced for a head-on collision. But suddenly he felt a funny sensation, as if he were on an elevator. His eyes flew open and he saw that SOPHIA 3rd was leaping over the robot's head. Eve's hand was closed around a lever marked EMERGENCY JUMP.

Jason let out a whoop of joy. "Way to go, Eve!"

"Don't count your turkeys before they're in the bush," Eve said, staring out the windshield.

Before Jason could figure that one out, he saw what Eve was looking at. Another, identical robot was headed their way.

"No sweat," Jason said. "We'll jump over this clodhopper, too!"

Eve looked into her rearview mirror. "No. They are both attacking now. We must blow them out."

"*Away!*" Jason said with panic in his voice. "Blow them *away!*"

"All right, I will," Eve said. She leaned over to Jason's control panel and pressed the button marked GUN.

With a sudden blast, a ball of light shot out of a gun port on SOPHIA 3rd's hood. The robot in front of them was instantly pulverized in a bright explosion.

Eve pulled a different lever, and the vehicle swiveled around. She leaned over and pressed GUN again.

Another flash of light, another robot bit the dust.

Jason heaved a sigh of relief. "So there is a weapon that works," he said.

"Yes," Eve replied, looking at the control panel. "You see, the power for the special weapons must be—"

"Look out!" Jason blurted. Eve had taken her eyes off the road, now SOPHIA 3rd was headed right for the drop-off.

It barged over the edge and began plummeting. Jason looked down and shrieked. Waiting at the bottom, bubbling furiously, was a pool of boiling lava!

CHAPTER 6

"No-o-o-o-o-o!" Jason shouted. He clamped his eyes shut and clenched his teeth.

"Oops," came Eve's voice.

The falling sensation stopped. Jason felt seasick, as if he'd just hit the bottom of a roller-coaster ride.

He opened one eye a bit. The sides of the cliff were still racing by — but now SOPHIA 3rd was going *up*.

It bounded over the top and landed on the second cliff.

"How did you do that?" Jason asked.

"To propel upward, SOPHIA 3rd must have contact with a solid or liquid underneath."

"You mean we touched that stuff at the bottom?" Jason said with disbelief.

"Briefly," Eve answered. "If we had stayed any longer, we might have been social studies."

"What?"

"Is that not a popular expression?"

Jason thought it out for a moment. "You mean, we might have been *history!*" He laughed. "I think I'm getting the hang of this."

Jason's good mood was short-lived. They floated over a ridge into a valley below — directly into the path of another robot.

"You know," Jason muttered, "these guys are getting annoying." He pressed GUN.

Blam! The robot disintegrated.

Jason smiled. "I think I'm getting the hang of this, too."

"Hang up...hang on...getting the hang of..." Eve murmured. "Your sling is quite confusing."

"Slang."

They came to another ridge, and Eve made the vehicle leap onto it. This time, when another robot came toward them, Jason didn't even blink.

"You're social studies, buddy!" he called out, pressing GUN again.

The robot exploded. "Yiii-hah!" Jason shouted with glee. "The coast is cl— "

The word caught in his throat. Where the robot had been standing, there was now a bright, pulsating sphere, the size of SOPHIA 3rd. "Uh, I lied," Jason said. "Stop, Eve."

But Eve didn't seem to hear him. She drove forward.

"Eve!" Jason warned. "Eve, don't you see the —"

But it was too late. Without slowing down, SOPHIA 3rd plowed into the sphere. There was a blinding burst of light.

Jason shut his eyes. "Eve, are you nuts?"

But the light lasted only a fraction of a second. When Jason opened his eyes again, he noticed the power gauge had increased.

"I did not intend to become . . . nuts," Eve said, frowning. "I have tried to attain a suitable human form."

"You have," Jason said. "Now can you tell me what just happened?"

"In this highly radioactive underworld, there is much that is not understood. Sometimes, for unknown reasons, a destroyed robot will leave a pocket of self-contained nuclear power."

"And if we drive through it, we absorb that power," Jason said.

"You are getting the hang of this!" Eve declared. "Now hang on!"

Four gaping holes lay in front of them, and Eve carefully guided SOPHIA 3rd over each one.

Around them on all sides, flying missiles whizzed by. "What is going on here?" Jason asked, his voice filled with exasperation.

Eve shifted into a low gear. In front of them was a long, dark tunnel. "We will be safe in here," she said. "I will explain all."

SOPHIA 3rd rolled into the tunnel. It was lit with a mysterious dull green, like the chamber Jason had first fallen into. He sat back and looked intently at Eve.

She took a deep breath. "My planet, Signar-el, was very tiny," she began. "There were many peaceful countries, all coexisting happily."

"You said 'was' and 'were,'" Jason commented. "Do you mean — "

"Please, Jason, I said I would explain all." Eve's eyes grew distant as memories began to flood her mind. "My father was the ruler of Poomblorg, the finest country on Signar-el. He was also the leading astroscientist on the planet, and he trained me well. I became the youngest winner of the Nova Red Prize for Science, for my theories of intergalactic life-forms."

"Congratulations," Jason interjected.

Eve gave a weak smile. "I'm afraid it makes no difference now. You see, I was on a mission to seek out alien life-forms, when I found your planet. Needless to say,

I was very happy. But when I transmitted the news to Signar-el, my commander's voice interrupted me. All he said was, 'Do not give your coordinates!' Then the line went dead. Unfortunately, it was too late. I had told them exactly where I was."

"What was wrong with that?" Jason asked.

"I had no idea—but I was more concerned with the signal blackout. I sped back to Signar-el, and all I saw—" her voice began to choke, and she wiped away a tear— "all I saw was a lifeless, glowing mass of radioactivity. The entire planet—every person, everything created during eons of civilization—had been destroyed!"

"I'm . . . I'm sorry," Jason said softly.

Eve sniffled, then went on: "As I approached Signar-el and tried to re-establish communication, there was a booming voice, so loud I had to cover my ears. I could not tell where it was coming from. It identified itself only as the Plutonium Boss. It laughed, and said it had found Signar-el to be a delightful home."

"It had been on your planet all along?"

"For thousands of years. Before that, it had been floating in space, dying for lack of its only food—plutonium."

"You mean that radioactive stuff they use to make atom bombs?" Jason asked.

"Yes. This so-called Plutonium Boss said that it had burrowed deep underneath Signar-el's crust ages ago, when we had first begun our nuclear age. We had just developed plutonium on a large scale."

"And it fed on the plutonium for years and years," Jason said.

Eve nodded. "It grew and grew like a cancer, hiding underground. Then, after it had stored enough, it burst through the surface, unleashing the power of three million atomic blasts. Signar-el was vaporized in an instant." Her eyes grew cold, and her jaw became set with anger. "It laughed as it told me this, and then . . . then it thanked me."

Jason was puzzled. "Thanked you for what?"

"For transmitting my coordinates to my commander." Eve turned and looked solemnly into Jason's eyes. "Now that Signar-el was used up, the evil creature's plutonium would decay quickly, sapping it of power. It would soon need another place to destroy. Another place that had plutonium. Another place where it could fester underground for ages. And after hearing my transmission, it knew it had found the perfect place."

Jason knew what she was going to say, but didn't want to hear it.

"My dear Jason," Eve said. "The Plutonium Boss is here, under the Earth, and we are going to find it."

GAME HINT

Use your cannon on the floating faces you encounter.

CHAPTER 7

Jason stared grimly forward. His brain was spinning. All he had meant to do was chase after a pet frog. Now, all of a sudden, he was in a race to save the world.

"It still doesn't make sense to me," he finally said. "Why was there a hole in the swamp, and what was that weird chest in it?"

"I do not know about the chest," Eve said. "But I do know that in order to breathe, the Plutonium Boss requires a certain swamp gas — methane, I believe."

"Is that the stuff that makes the swamp smell so bad?"

"To the Plutonium Boss, that smell is like perfume."

Jason scrunched up his nose. "It figures."

"The hole you came down is one of the Plutonium Boss's blowholes," Eve said. "For some reason, swamp creatures have been attracted to these holes — especially frogs. Several have fallen in."

"But why?"

Eve shrugged. "Batters me."

"Uh, I think you mean, beats me," Jason said. He sighed. "And you were speaking so well, Eve!"

"I am sorry," Eve said. "Please bore with me."

"*Bear!*" Jason corrected.

Eve looked around. "A bear? Where?"

"No, no." Jason laughed. "You know, sometimes I think you're putting me on."

"Putting you on what?"

Groaning, Jason shook his head. "Never mind!"

Eve ignored him, concentrating on the road. Before long, she pointed out the windshield at a distant pinpoint of light. "We are almost at the end. Please be careful. This is where the other human got lost."

Jason stared at her. "Other human?"

"I neglected to tell you about him. His name was Alex."

"*Was?* What happened to him?"

"I do not know. On one of his solo energy-seeking missions, he never returned to the vehicle. I can only assume he was a casualty of the Plutonium Boss."

"Oh, great." Jason gulped. "And, uh, what is a solo energy-seeking mission?"

"You will find out."

Before Jason could react, SOPHIA 3rd

zoomed out the other end of the tunnel. Suddenly the ground beneath them disappeared.

The vehicle flew through the air, landing with a dull bump. Around them was a dark grotto. The dirt walls were covered with green moss, and a heavy smell of mildew hung in the air.

"Okay, what kind of place have you taken me to now?" Jason demanded.

"Greetings!"

"Yeeeagh!" Jason cried out, covering his ears. The voice was so loud, he felt his seat vibrate.

"Plutonium Boss, do not think you can scare us!" Eve shouted. "It is *you* who must fear *us!*"

A low, rumbling laughter began. The walls around them shook with its rhythm.

"Don't egg him on!" Jason whispered.

"Do not worry," Eve reassured him. "There are no eggs on this vehicle at all."

"Yeah," Jason replied, shuddering. "Just one big chicken!"

The laughter swelled, until moss began to shake loose from the walls. Jason thought there might be an earthquake.

It stopped abruptly, and the voice spoke again:

"Welcome to the underground;
Please feel free to turn around.
But should you choose to forge ahead,
Heed this: the tour ends when you're dead!
The traps are set for fools who dare:
A dozen levels, save two pair.
To find your host, Plutonium Boss,
First go down, and then across,
Thence to your death — and this planet's loss!"

The laughter welled up again, then faded.

Jason heard a clattering noise below him. "What's that?" he exclaimed.

"I believe it is your feet," Eve replied.

Jason looked down to see his boots shaking against the metal floor of SOPHIA 3rd. "I think . . . I think we should leave."

"You do not want to find Fred? You do not want to save the Earth?"

Jason swallowed hard. "Sure . . . sure. But where are we supposed to go?"

"I do not know. Perhaps there were clues in the poem."

Jason thought back, remembering the words. " 'A dozen levels, save two pair.' Let's see, two pairs are four, so that's twelve minus four — eight levels! There must be eight levels in this underworld."

"Ah, *now* we are speaking!" Eve said. "But what did he mean by going down, and then across?"

Jason scanned the area. A few feet in front of them, a large hole dropped downward into blackness. "Let's try that," he said.

Eve took a deep breath. "I suppose we must. It is like that saying: When the going gets tough, the tough go away."

"Uh, right," Jason said. "Just drive, before I realize what a dumb idea this is."

With a *whoosh*, SOPHIA 3rd moved forward and dropped into the hole.

Jason's body strained upward against the shoulder harness. Outside the window was nothing but blackness. He felt as if he were in an elevator whose cable had snapped.

Near the bottom, Eve pulled a lever marked LANDING THRUSTERS. SOPHIA 3rd slowed down and touched the ground gently.

Jason heaved a sigh of relief. "You always do have something up your sleeve, don't you?"

"Of course," Eve replied, looking at him as if he were crazy. "My arm."

Ahead of them was a long, narrow corridor, just wide enough for SOPHIA 3rd. Eve edged forward. In the murky light, Jason spotted a rotting sign attached to the wall. It said LEVEL 2 and pointed straight ahead.

"Piece of cake," Jason remarked. "I wonder if they'll all be this easy to find."

"Sheeeeeeeeeeeeeeee!"

A piercing shriek made Jason's hair stand on end. SOPHIA 3rd rolled out the end of the passageway and into a high, narrow chamber. Eve slammed on the brake.

"What is that thing?" was all Jason could say.

Standing in front of a thick wooden door was a guard. Its eyes stared at them from high above, and when its mouth opened, its chin scraped the ground.

It was a head.

No legs, no arms, no torso. No body.

All Jason and Eve could do was stare in shock, then three deadly missiles shot out of its mouth!

CHAPTER 8

Sshhhhhpokkkk!

SOPHIA 3rd lurched backward from the force of the hit. The power gauge dipped a full notch.

Sshhhhhpokkkk!!

The vehicle jumped backward again. It was at the edge of the tunnel now, and the power gauge was dangerously low. "Fire back!" Eve shouted.

Jason drummed his finger on GUN, as fast as he could. A barrage of bullets shot toward the guard's open mouth.

Thwack, thwack, thwack, thwack, thwack, thwack, thwack, thwack!

It was as if Jason were throwing popcorn in its mouth. The guard just swallowed the gunfire.

Sshhhhhpokkkk! came the guard's return blast.

SOPHIA 3rd was thrown clear back into the tunnel.

"We need better weapons!" Eve shouted. "Let's get out of here!"

She put SOPHIA 3rd in reverse and sped back along the narrow tunnel. Jason looked at the dashboard. The power gauge was almost at zero.

Eve was looking, too. "We were almost dead beets," she said.

Jason nodded. "Dead meat."

"No, dead beets," Eve responded. "I am a vegetarian."

She tapped Jason's weapon panel. "Our mission is going to be treacherous. We must activate these weapons if we are to survive."

"But how?"

"In the underworld, there are many small chambers that SOPHIA 3rd will not fit into. One person must go in, alone. These chambers contain the energy capsules necessary to power our weapons."

"Hey, I'm there!" Jason said. "Just point the way."

"But I must warn you. These chambers are also full of deadly traps."

"Oh." Jason suddenly lost his enthusiasm.

SOPHIA 3rd zoomed out of the tunnel. Jason breathed a sigh of relief.

Until he saw what was in front of them.

It was a cavern — no, worse than that, it was a nightmare of a cavern. Its walls loomed high above as far as the eye could see. Screams and shrieks echoed around them, sounding like needles scraping across records. Strange mechanical birds swooped down, releasing missiles of explosive energy.

Along the walls there were long, flat ledges. Each one was patrolled by a robot exactly like the ones Eve and Jason had vanquished earlier.

And directly in front of them, a sea of black water stretched out. The surface was covered with large bubbles. But when Jason looked closer, he saw they weren't bubbles at all. They were glowing, radioactive jellyfish.

"Eve," Jason said, "take us to one of those chambers. Anything would be better than this!"

Eve propelled SOPHIA 3rd onto one of the ledges — directly into the path of a robot.

"Is this the way to a chamber, Eve?" Jason asked. The robot came closer. "Eve, what are we doing here?"

"Fire, Jason!" Eve shouted.

"No kidding!" Jason destroyed the robot, and a power orb hung in the air.

Eve steered the vehicle through the orb. The power gauge went up a notch.

Jason smiled. "I get it. You want to

power back up to full before we go on!"

"You are really on the bat, Jason!"

"And you're on the ball!" Jason answered.

Eve guided SOPHIA 3rd from ledge to ledge. Jason shot down robots and mechanical birds until the power gauge was full.

When SOPHIA 3rd landed on a high, quiet ledge, Jason hollered with joy. "We made it!"

"Yes," Eve said. "Now would you like to go, or shall I?"

"Go?" Jason looked out the window. A narrow door was concealed in the wall of the cavern. "Is that one of the chambers?"

"Yes. One of us must venture inside. The other will stay with SOPHIA 3rd."

Jason thought about it for a moment. "Eve, you're the one who knows how to operate this vehicle. I think I should go."

"A wise choice." She reached into a compartment under her seat and took out a small gun. "Take this laser blaster. With this, your helmet, and your wits, you will be protected."

Jason knew if he didn't act fast, he might change his mind. He clutched the gun in one hand, and opened the door with the other. "Thank you, Eve. I'll be back."

"Don't take any wooden pickles."

"Nickels."

"Those either," Eve replied. "Good luck."

Jason gave her a salute. He turned to the door, tightened his fingers around the gun, and pushed his way through.

Immediately he wished he hadn't.

Voooooozh! The moment he stepped into the room, he had to duck a flying missile. He tried to stand up, but another one just grazed his helmet.

Jason quickly backed into the chamber doorway, where the barrage of missiles couldn't reach him. He took a close look at what was throwing them.

He almost gagged. It was a one-eyed metallic blob with a coat of long steel-wool hair. The missiles were flying around it in a wide circle, like bola balls.

Jason knew there was no turning back. For the sake of Fred, for the sake of the world. He lifted his laser gun and fired.

Beeoo-beeoo-beeoo-beeoo-beeoo!

With a bang that shook the chamber, the creature disappeared. The only thing left was a thick wall of cement blocks.

"Energy capsules," he muttered to himself, looking around. "I don't even know what energy capsules look like."

He walked into the chamber, hoping

they would appear magically. Nothing happened.

Out of frustration, he took a shot at the wall.

Beeoo!

Instantly a huge cement block turned to dust, leaving a gaping hole. Behind it, Jason could see another section of the chamber.

Could it be the capsules were behind the wall? Jason squeezed through the hole to the other side and looked around.

Nothing.

He sighed. Maybe Eve should have come in after all. She would know where to look. He trudged back toward the hole, firing off two more rounds for target practice.

Beeoo-beeoo-beeoo!

Two cement blocks vanished, leaving no trace.

Beeoo!

There it was — right where the third block had been. It was a radiant sphere of energy. Inside it was a hologram of a fearsome electronic weapon.

"Eureka!" Jason exclaimed. He walked toward it, hand outstretched. It shimmered when his fingertips touched it. With a strange electronic whimper, it disappeared. Jason felt his suit receiving its energy.

Jason blasted his way through every block of the wall. There were three more capsules, and he picked up the energy from each one.

Feeling a surge of power, Jason ran out of the chamber. Eve was waiting patiently in SOPHIA 3rd near the edge of a cliff. He leapt into the air, landing right near the vehicle.

"Eve!" he yelled. "Guess what I—"

But those were the only words he could say. The edge of the cliff gave out beneath him. He felt his body slip off.

With a scream of terror, he looked downward. The murky darkness of the lagoon rushed toward him. In it, the radioactive jellyfish seemed to be quivering.

With delight.

CHAPTER 9

Jason fell into the dark water with a loud splash. Down, down he sank beneath the surface. He held his breath for a moment — until he realized he didn't have to. His suit and helmet protected him from the water.

But not from the glowing jellyfish.

They came at him, bubbling and beeping. With each pulsation, their tentacles shot out and then back in again.

Jason had never been a good swimmer, but today he felt ready for the Olympics. He kicked hard and propelled himself backward. The jellyfish were slow to respond. Relieved, Jason flipped around and began to do an underwater dog paddle.

And came face to face with another pack of jellyfish.

He looked above and below. More jellyfish! They were closing in on him like a swarm of bees.

There was no place to go. A shout raced toward Jason's lips, but he held it back.

Down here, no one would hear him. Down here, it would be a quick, silent, cold death.

A tentacle glided toward him. He lurched backward.

"Yeeeeow!" The tip of the tentacle brushed his suit. A jolt pierced through him. It felt like a lightning bolt.

He wriggled right and left, barely avoiding tentacles. He scrunched his shoulders and pinned his arms to his side.

And that's when he felt the gun.

He hadn't thought of it, hadn't imagined that it might work underwater. He still wasn't sure it would.

He ripped it out of his holster and took aim.

B-l-o-o-o-o, b-l-o-o-o, b-l-o-o-o-o-o . . .

The noise was muffled underwater, but the laser darts made contact.

Plooooomf! A jellyfish disappeared, leaving a small whirlpool.

Then another disappeared, and another. Jason's aim was perfect. One by one, he picked them off.

"Yeee-*hah!*" he yelled, feeling like a gunslinger in an old Western.

It was time to get to the surface and find Eve. By now he had sunk so low, the water was almost pitch-black. He thrust powerfully with his arms and kicked.

He felt as if he were standing still. He thrust and kicked again.

This time he knew he wasn't standing still. The coral formations on the wall were rising — which meant he was *sinking!*

It was the suit, he knew it. It was made for land travel, and it was too heavy to use underwater. He started to take it off, then stopped himself. The suit was the only thing keeping him from drowning.

Helplessly, he flailed in the water, until he suddenly stopped moving.

There was something beneath him. Something gooey.

He planted both feet. They sank a few inches, but stayed put. He took a few steps, expecting to plunge off a ledge. If only he could see . . .

As if in answer, a flock of beeping jellyfish appeared to his left. Their glow cast dull light around them. Jason could see he was at the bottom of the lagoon. He grabbed his gun and fired.

One by one, the jellyfish exploded, sending out bursts of light. And in the last burst, Jason saw something that gave him hope.

A ladder.

Lifting his feet gingerly out of the muck, Jason trudged blindly onward. He kept his hands in front of him, feeling for the ladder.

When his fingers closed around a wooden rung, he began to climb.

And climb . . . and climb . . .

The farther he got from the bottom, the less dark it was. He stopped counting the steps at three hundred. By then, he could see the top — a tiny ledge jutting out of the wall, just above the water.

There was barely enough room on it to stand. On the wall, covered by a thick film of seaweed and algae, there was a small door. It was either go through the door or go back down the ladder. It took about a half second to make the choice.

Jason ripped the seaweed away and pulled the door open. He stepped inside and cautiously looked around.

There was a maze of pathways, formed by a twisting hedge of plants. He carefully followed along the hedge, going left and right, trying to see what was ahead of him. Never once did he look behind.

And that was his first mistake.

When the blast hit him, it was from behind. He felt himself jerk forward, but he never felt himself hit the floor. By that time, everything had gone completely black!

CHAPTER 10

"Ughhhh . . ." Jason moaned. He had gone unconscious, and for a moment he had forgotten why.

The second blast reminded him.

It hurt like crazy. He scrambled to his feet and turned. A tiny metal machine was rolling toward him. It was shaped like a gumdrop — except Jason had never seen a gumdrop with a gun turret on its head.

Jason fired a quick blast from his laser gun.

Plooooomf! came the muffled explosion.

"You are now an *ex*-gumdrop, pal," he said.

Keeping his gun out, he continued onward. He turned a sharp corner, and vanquished two other gumdrop robots.

He clung to the hedge, inching along a narrow corridor. At the end he had to take a sharp left. There the path was cut off by a cement-block wall.

"Piece of cake," he said to himself,

blasting his way through. Just as he expected, some of the blocks contained weapon capsules. He stopped at each one, absorbing the energy into his suit.

He wasn't sure what he was going to do with that energy or how he would transfer it to the SOPHIA 3rd control board. But he'd worry about that later.

The pathway was blocked by more walls, and Jason blasted through every one. Finally he came to the other side of the cavern and realized what he had come all this way to see.

Another door.

With an exasperated grunt, Jason kicked it open.

Clannng ... Clanng ... Clanng ...

It felt as if someone were banging a gong in his ears. He cringed and backed toward the door.

"Greetings, my friend. You made it," came the same booming voice Jason and Eve had heard before.

Jason looked around, but there was nothing but an empty chamber. "What's the matter, you ran out of rhymes?" he asked out loud, mustering up his bravery.

"It's difficult to feel poetic when I am preparing for a kill."

The words sent a shiver up Jason's spine. "I'm not afraid of you," he retorted.

He was lying.

"**My robots weren't afraid of you, and look at what happened to them. I have had enough of your kind. Prepare to die.**"

Jason lifted his laser gun. "Easy for you to say, swamp breath!"

A low rumble began. It seemed to come from within the walls and below the ground. Jason thought it was an earthquake — but as the noise got louder, he realized he was wrong.

It was laughter. Sinister, ugly laughter that sliced through Jason like a knife. "Wh-where are you?" he cried out. He was starting to shake. "I-I'll g-get you, Plutonium Boss!"

The laughter became a wild, bellowing cackle. Jason whirled around, trying to spot something, anything.

Then the chamber fell into darkness. The laughter swelled louder. Jason couldn't stand it another minute. He reared back his head and let out a scream that ripped his vocal cords.

"No-o-o-o-o-o-o-o-o-o-o-o-o!"

And when he opened his eyes, he was momentarily blinded.

But in that flash of light, he had glimpsed his enemy. The sight alone was almost enough to make him pass out. He covered his eyes and staggered backward. He couldn't think, could barely move. And even though he wasn't looking, he could feel it was coming toward him.

"**I'll let you take one more glance,**" said his enemy, "**and then I shall blow you off the face of the earth.**"

GAME HINT

After you defeat the first Underboss, destroy the wall guard to get to Level 2.

CHAPTER 11

Jason slumped to the ground. He tried to take his arms away from his face, struggling to look at the dreadful *thing* before him.

Suddenly he was yanked off his feet. He flew in the air and landed several feet away.

His head throbbed. His body was screaming with pain. He gasped for the breath that had been knocked out of him.

He could no longer afford to cover his eyes. He had to see what was attacking him.

Lifting his aching head, he looked straight at his adversary for the first time. His body tensed with the shock.

It wasn't the glare — his eyes had adjusted to that. It was the sheer ugliness.

One minute it looked like an enormous, bloated mass of animal blubber. The next minute it looked like pictures of a tumor Jason had seen in a magazine. But it was alive, its lumpy skin palpitating like a human heart. Limp feelers hung like hairs of a scraggly beard. Its color was a putrid greenish-yellow. As it throbbed, it turned to red and gave out a groaning sound, along with a sickening *squish, squish*.

Fireballs orbited around it at lightning speed. They came within inches of Jason, and he scrabbled away. He realized it must have been one of those that had thrown him into the air.

"Have a little laser fire, you mutant!" Jason said. He aimed his gun and pulled the trigger.

The laughter welled up again. **"What was that? Did I feel a change in the wind?"** the mutant blob thundered.

Jason fired again and again. Each time, the laser ricocheted off an invisible shield formed by the orbiting fireballs.

As long as Jason was outside the orbit, he knew his shots would never penetrate. Would he be able to get inside the orbit? Would that work?

There was only one way to find out. Stepping quickly, Jason walked toward the mutant. The fireballs' orbit changed constantly, rising and falling. Sometimes it was at eye level, sometimes it rose high into the air. He waited patiently for the right moment, watching the fireballs *whoosh* by with blinding speed.

When the moment was right, he rushed in.

B-l-o-o-o-o-o, b-l-o-o-o-o, b-l-o-o-o-o-o!

This time the shots met their mark. The blob glowed bright white and swelled. It let out a high-pitched squeal. Jason was inches away from it now. He could feel the intense heat through his suit. Behind him, the fireballs were changing orbit. Their flames were beginning to lick at his helmet.

He turned around and dove into the air. With a perfect commando roll, he landed on the ground and ran safely away.

"I have been too nice to you," the creature boomed. **"Now I shall crush you like a mosquito!"**

Pulsing furiously, the blob came closer. Jason jumped away. His back slammed against a dirt wall. He slid against the wall, moving to the right. The creature came after him. Jason groped with his hands, not daring to turn around, hoping to feel a corridor opening. He never did.

Instead, he found a corner.

"Uh-oh," was all he could say.

The creature roared with laughter. **"Feeling cozy, I hope?"**

There was no place to go — but forward. Jason lunged toward the creature, screaming a war cry at the top of his lungs: "Die, Plutonium Boss!"

He barely missed being clobbered by a fireball. Stepping inside the orbit, he let loose with a barrage of laser fire.

The creature swelled and glowed bright white. Screeching, it tried to move away. It twisted and lurched, attempting to pull the fireballs inward.

Jason copied it, move for move. His gritted teeth showed bright white within his helmet. His index finger clamped tightly onto the trigger.

Now the creature was frantic. When it swelled, it gave off a horrendous odor, like the swamp. Its raging skin bubbled at Jason, charring his sleeves.

B-l-o-o-o-o-o!

With an earsplitting crash, Jason was hurled backward. Once again, he slammed against the wall. Intense pain ripped through him, followed by naked terror. A fireball must have hit him from behind. He thought he heard an explosion, but it was probably the ring of pain in his ears. The Plutonium Boss would be mad, real mad — and this time, there would be no mercy.

He bolted upright and faced the creature. Gripping the gun with two arms, he held it rock-steady and shot blindly.

The laser streaked across the room and buried itself in the opposite wall.

Jason dropped his arms. The room was empty.

He could see the air pulsing with the spent energy of a destroyed radioactive mutant.

"I . . . I did it," Jason whispered, as if to convince himself. Then louder: "I did it!" He dropped to his knees and began shaking with uncontrollable laughter. "I, Jason Frudnick, killed the Plutonium Boss!"

He ran through the door and ran back through the other chamber. When he saw another gumdrop robot, he vanquished it with a behind-the-back shot. At the other end, he opened the door and stepped out onto the ledge. All he had to do now was find Eve.

Maybe that wouldn't be too hard. He fired a laser beam into the air, tracing a wide circle. He did it to the left and the right. If Eve were looking for him, she'd be sure to see it.

He was right. Within minutes, SOPHIA 3rd appeared on a ledge above him. As he stepped back into the doorwell, Eve maneuvered the vehicle onto the ledge.

Her door flew open. "Any luck?" she asked. "Did you get some weapon power?"

Jason grinned triumphantly. "We're not going to need it."

"I beg your pardon?" Eve said, eyeing him curiously.

Bubbling with excitement, Jason grabbed her arms. "Eve, I got him!"

"Got him?" A look of astonishment washed across Eve's face. "You don't mean you killed the Plutonium Boss?"

"That's exactly what he means!" came an earthshaking voice.

Jason felt his stomach clench. The cavern shook with the Plutonium Boss's grim laughter.

CHAPTER 12

"Who are you?" Jason called out into the void.

"Who do you think I am?" the voice thundered. The ledge shook with the vibrations, and Jason and Eve clung to each other.

The voice was different — deeper, more menacing. Jason couldn't help but tremble at the sound of it. "But — but I...I destroyed you!"

The laugh turned into a high-pitched shriek. Clods of mud and fungus dislodged from the cavern walls and began raining around them. Electrical sparks zigzagged through the air like lightning.

When the shriek stopped, the voice bellowed angrily: **"You thought that piffling pile of putrescent protoplasm was me? You thought that I, the Plutonium Boss, would let myself be outfought by a half-witted child?"**

"W-well...I th-thought—" Jason stammered.

"Silence! I'll do the thinking here! The defective tub of lard you defeated was merely a Mutant Underboss. Being the weakest one I owned, he guarded the first level. So save your bragging, you simpering slush brain. There are seven more deadly levels, six more Underbosses between me and you. Somehow, I don't think we shall ever have the pleasure of meeting!"

The voice let out a cackling roar, then faded away.

Silence hung in the air. Then slowly, the distant cavern noises resumed: robots clomping, wings batting, strange liquids dripping, electronic noises humming.

"This is not going to be easy, Jason," Eve said. It was the understatement of the year.

Jason knew he should be quaking with fright. He knew he should hop into SOPHIA 3rd and beg Eve to take him home.

But something had changed Jason. Something about the way the Plutonium Boss had talked to him. Something about the sureness, the cockiness — the idea that Jason could be treated like a speck of dust.

No one treated Jason Frudnick like that. And no one called him a simpering slush brain.

"Eve," he said, his jaw set firm, "I will fight to the last breath. For Fred — for the planet. If the Plutonium Boss is going to succeed, it won't be because I didn't try."

Eve beamed. "You are a real sandwich on a long roll, Jason!"

"Hero," Jason said, too hyped-up to laugh.

"Sorry," Eve said. "You are a real sandwich on a long hero!"

"Skip it," Jason replied. "Let's go."

He hopped into the passenger seat, and Eve took her place behind the wheel. Eve propelled SOPHIA 3rd from ledge to ledge. They hopped into the paths of robots, they were attacked by swooping mechanical birds, they fell into the lagoon and fought jellyfish.

Through it all, Eve guided the vehicle and Jason shot down enemies one by one.

Within minutes, they were traveling down the tunnel to the bodiless door guard. Jason flexed his fingers, preparing for the onslaught.

Eve gave his weapon panel a gentle tap. "You'll be able to use this now," she said. "The weapons should be powered up by now."

"But I didn't do anything," Jason said. "I mean, I picked up the energy, but I didn't transfer it."

"Ah, but you did automatically, as soon as you stepped into SOPHIA 3rd. You see, the vehicle's inner force field has been set to a constant flux between the occupant and the weapon reserve — sort of like an inductance coil."

"Uh, right," Jason said. "I think I understand you better when you're tripping over slang expressions."

"Never mind," Eve said. "I recommend that you greet our big-mouthed friend with the multiwarhead missile."

Jason set his finger over the correct control.

This time, when they entered the chamber, Jason let the weapon fly.

Ffffoshhhh-ffffoshhhh-ffffoshhhh!

With each blast, three flaming projectiles shot out of SOPHIA 3rd. They flew directly into the gaping mouth of the door guard.

The guard's eyes widened in shock. He swallowed the missiles, sent out a few of his own, and then blew up.

"No sweat," Jason said.

"Onward to Level Two!" Eve cried out.

She drove through the door. SOPHIA 3rd sped through another dark tunnel, then plunged out the other side.

The vehicle's engine echoed loudly in this chamber. Instead of dirt and moss, the walls were solid, curved metal. It felt like they were in a huge pipe with a diameter the size of a football field.

"Great," Jason said. "All that, and we end up in the sewer!"

Cllllllang!

SOPHIA 3rd bounced on its shocks. Its roof reverberated from a sudden hit.

"Roof rockets!" Eve shouted.

"How do I shoot them?" Jason demanded.

"I'll tell you in a minute!" Eve replied. "Let's get out of—"

Suddenly Jason braced himself. "Look out for the lava pit!" he yelled.

Directly in SOPHIA 3rd's path was a bubbling pool of red-hot molten rock. One second of contact and their vehicle would be sizzled to a crisp.

Eve's index finger darted toward the EMERGENCY JUMP button. Just as the front wheels rolled over the edge, SOPHIA 3rd lifted sharply upward toward the roof.

Jason breathed a sigh of relief. "Eve, you're a genius!"

But Eve's face was turning a pale shade of white. "Uh-oh," she murmured, her eyes fixed upward. "I think I may have pressed a little too hard."

Jason followed her glance. A forest of gleaming, knife-sharp blades hung from the ceiling. And judging from the vehicle's speed, there was no way they were going to avoid it.

"Duck!" Jason yelled. As if that would do any good.

With a fierce *screeeeeek* of shredding metal, three long spikes ripped through the roof above Jason and Eve.

GAME HINT

Once you get started,
go straight to the ocean.

CHAPTER 13

Jason pulled Eve down to the floor. The spikes tore deeper into the roof, inching toward them with sickening slowness. Jason and Eve sank further, scrunching their bodies into a nearly impossible position. Their frightened eyes were like four enormous white globes. The points edged closer. Jason could feel the pores of his skin closing up.

Scrockkk! With a last wrenching noise, the spikes stopped. One of the points was inches from Jason's nose. He stared at it, cross-eyed. "Eve," he said, "whatever you do, don't let me breathe."

He grabbed the spike with his hand. Slowly he angled his body around the point, until he was sitting in the passenger seat. Eve did the same, edging her way into the driver's seat.

To see her, Jason had to look around three of the spikes. "Now what?" he asked.

Eve examined the ceiling. "Severe damage. We must somehow get down and repair this."

"How about firing some of our weapons?" Jason suggested. "The recoil might shake us off the ceiling."

"A creative suggestion. But we must not waste our weapon energy. Like a battery, it can be used up."

"Okay, then how about a little rock and roll?" Jason said.

Eve frowned. "There is no radio in SOPHIA 3rd."

Jason began shaking forward and backward in his seat. "I mean this kind of rock and roll!"

Together they lurched back and forth, and SOPHIA 3rd began to rock.

Reeek, reeek, reeek, reeek, reeek . . . The serrated edges of the spikes held fast.

"We're only making the holes bigger!" Eve said, looking at the gaps in the roof.

"That'll help us," Jason replied. He reached for the MULTIWARHEAD MISSILE button. "There's no other way. I'm going to use some weapon energy. Hang tight!"

A barrage shot out of the gun turret. SOPHIA 3rd jerked backward. With an agonizing *scrrrroooockkk,* it pulled loose from the spikes and began hurtling to the ground.

"Brilliant!" Eve said as she guided the vehicle to a safe landing. Avoiding traps, she maneuvered SOPHIA 3rd onto an empty ledge. There, she and Jason got a hammer out of the trunk and banged the torn metal back upward into the roof.

There were still holes, but they were smaller. Minor damage compared to what would have happened if SOPHIA 3rd had landed in the lava pit.

They sped away at top speed. Here in the second level, there were side rooms, too. Jason stopped at these and picked up more weapon power.

It was in one of these rooms that Jason met the second Mutant Underboss.

Clannng ... Clanng ... Clanng ...

The sound was familiar, and this time Jason had more gunpower. He braced himself for the flying fireballs, for the hideous mass of protoplasm.

"Come out, Underboss!" he shouted bravely. "I'm ready for you!"

"Are you sure?" answered the powerful voice of the Plutonium Boss.

The sound jarred Jason. His confidence slipped. But he thought of poor Fred, who must have been suffering a horrible fate, if he was still alive. He thought of the innocent world above, where his friends and family were probably just now waking up to a gorgeous day. He thought about beaches, and trees, and ice cream, and video games, and books, and ten-speed bikes. And he knew he had to stand his ground against the warped mind that wanted to take it all away.

"Sure I'm sure," he said with firm control. "Throw whatever you've got at me. I'm not running away."

Laughter exploded around him. **"Then you're a bigger fool than I thought!"** roared the Plutonium Boss.

There was a flash of light. Jason shut his eyes but remained still. When he opened them, his enemy was facing him.

He gulped. His grip loosened around his gun. There were no fireballs. There was no mass of protoplasm at all.

Instead, there was a crab. A towering, grotesque crab, crouched and ready to jump.

The laughter bubbled up again. **"I knew you'd like him,"** said the Plutonium Boss. **"I understand you have a weakness for obnoxious little animals."**

Jason shaded his eyes from the grotesque, overgrown creature. "You can't scare me!" he called out.

He pelted the crab with laser fire. It reached out to Jason, snapping with its claws. Jason rolled out of the way, springing to his feet and firing again.

The crab took the hit, then opened its mouth. For a moment Jason thought it would scream in pain. But it didn't make a sound.

Three spheres, like cannonballs, flew out of its mouth. Jason ducked. One of the spheres hit the wall next to him. It exploded, sending shards of metal into the air.

Jason fell to his stomach. He held his laser gun with both arms extended in front of him. The crab monster swung its claws toward toward him. Jason took aim again.

Beeoo-beeoo-beeoo-beeoo-beeoo!

The crab monster exploded. It echoed against the metal walls of the chamber, making the room shake violently. Jason was tossed backward. Acrid greenish-yellow smoke billowed up from where the crab had been.

Jason leapt to his feet. He felt wrenched apart inside. It wasn't because of the tossing about, or the smoke, or the bruises all over him.

It was because he imagined that somewhere in the Plutonium Boss's world, Fred might be waiting. Not the gentle pet Jason missed so much — but a hideous monster like the crab, transformed by the Boss. Could it be?

"Where are you keeping Fred?" Jason's voice was an anguished shout. It echoed emptily in the cavernous room.

In the silence that followed, Jason had a terrifying thought. Maybe the Plutonium Boss didn't know who Fred was. Maybe Fred was just another pest that the Boss had mutated or killed according to his whims.

After what seemed like hours, the Plutonium Boss answered. His tone was gentle and soft, which somehow made it absolutely bone-chilling.

"Your Fred is doing very well," the Plutonium Boss said. **"Yes, indeed. Very, very well!"**

GAME HINT

When fighting the ladybugs, shoot them as they come around the corner.

CHAPTER 14

Jason felt light-headed, as if he were going to be sick. It had something to do with the Plutonium Boss's voice. The words were reassuring, but the meaning behind them wasn't. He wanted to feel relieved that Fred was alive, but he didn't.

He hated to think it, but even death might be better than falling under the control of the Plutonium Boss.

Jason shook those thoughts out of his head. He couldn't afford to stand still at a time like this. Blasting his way back through the room, he found the door and stepped outside.

At that precise moment, Eve rolled by in SOPHIA 3rd. She was going slowly enough so that Jason could pull open his door and hop in.

"I got him," he said, landing in his seat. "Let's go to the next level."

Eve didn't answer. She looked straight ahead as SOPHIA 3rd continued its slow course.

Jason settled into his seat. Eve must have been fatigued, and he didn't blame her. After all, she'd been down here fighting much longer than he had. He had to admire her, and he had to respect her feelings if she wanted to be quiet for a while.

Still, it seemed a little strange that she wasn't accelerating at all. But Jason trusted Eve enough to know she had something up her sleeve — besides arms.

As they approached another lava pit, Jason didn't flinch. Now that they knew what to expect, Eve would simply make the vehicle leap over it. All she had to do was reach out and push the EMERGENCY JUMP button. Out of the corner of his eye, he watched her right hand. It wasn't moving.

SOPHIA 3rd rumbled forward. Its front wheels rolled over the lip of the pit.

"Eve!" Jason shouted. "What is wrong with you?"

He eyed the button, which was on the left side of Eve's control panel. He would have to reach across her to get to it. Instinctively his arm darted out.

As it did, it passed right through her, as if she were a ghost!

CHAPTER 15

"Aaaaagh!" Jason cried out.

At the same time, his finger pressed the button. SOPHIA 3rd leapt over the lava pit in the nick of time.

"Eve!" Stupified, Jason stared at her expressionless face. She just stared ahead, unseeing, unhearing. He felt like he was looking at a movie of Eve, not the real thing. "Eve?"

He tried to touch her, but his hand passed through again. He snapped his fingers inches from her eyes, but she didn't blink.

Slowly he felt his shock transforming into anger. "You *can't* answer, can you?" he said. "Because you're not Eve at all. You're some kind of image, some kind of — "

"**Hologram?**" blared the Plutonium Boss's evil voice. "**Hope you didn't mind my filling in the word for you. I was getting impatient. How does it feel to be all alone in the underworld, Jason?**"

Jason twisted his way into the driver's seat and took control of SOPHIA 3rd. "Where is Eve?" he said.

"**What fun would it be if I told you?**" the Plutonium Boss replied. "**Clearly you enjoy this game of searching around. I've just made it a little more challenging.**"

Fury welled up inside Jason. First Fred, and now Eve. It wasn't fair. "Why don't you take me instead, you blowhard?" Jason shouted. "Go ahead! Return Eve and Fred, and take me. Let's just forget about the six other levels — I'll give you a fight right now! What's the matter, are you afraid?"

"**Hoooooo-ha-ha-ha-ha-ha!**" Once again, the cavern shook with thunderous laughter. "**Afraid? You are still suffering from delusions! Precisely the opposite — the reason I haven't taken you is because you humans are too frail! I need tough species, ones that I can mutate into new forms that serve my needs. The last time I tried that on a human, he fell apart. You consider yourselves the most advanced form of life — Ha! I have much more success with amphibians — and, of course, natives of that hearty planet, Signar-el!**"

The words hit Jason with sledge-hammer force. They toughened his resolve, steeled him for the lonely battle ahead. "All right, you warped has-been," he hissed. "If that's the way you want it, fine. I'll see you at Level Eight!"

"More delusions!" the Plutonium Boss screamed. His laughter became shrill and high-pitched, boomeranging around Jason like the howls of caged hyenas.

He forged onward. Within minutes, he had figured out the controls for SOPHIA 3rd. Level 3 whizzed by in a hail of laser blasts and vaporizing robots. There, he was attacked by a group of eight killer robots. Keeping his wits about him, Jason defeated them after a long battle.

In Level 4, Jason felt a rush of energy. When he got past this level, he would be halfway. He raced from room to room, leaving SOPHIA 3rd when he needed to collect weapon power. The vehicle's power was becoming awesome. It could shoot in all directions. It could hover for long periods of time. It could climb walls and ride along the ceiling. And it could fire bullets that took curved paths to follow moving targets.

The Level 4 Underboss was a frog that hopped wildly around him. Jason looked closely. It wasn't Fred, that was easy enough to see. It was a different breed, a grotesque and overgrown bullfrog, not the mild-mannered species that Jason knew so well.

A long tongue lashed out of its mouth, glowing with deadly nuclear energy. Jason hopped aside and bombarded it.

When the frog monster disintegrated in a blaze of smoke, Jason fell to his knees. It was time to rest. His muscles were tight with fatigue. He sat on a twisted metallic piece of debris and stared at the floor.

And at something that looked very definitely like an arm.

A human arm, sticking out from a half-open door.

Suddenly Jason wasn't tired. He ran to the door and yanked it open.

He stared in disbelief. He reached down to make sure what he was seeing wasn't a hologram.

It wasn't. His hand made contact with a protective suit just like his own.

Inside the suit, his head tilted lifelessly to one side, was a boy.

A boy Jason knew.

CHAPTER 16

"Alex?" The name escaped Jason's mouth before he had time to think.

Eve had mentioned someone named Alex, but Jason had no idea it was this Alex.

The slightly lopsided nose, the frizzy hair, the eyebrows that almost came together in the middle — even through the helmet, Alex Bufoni's features stood out. The last time Jason had seen him was two weeks ago in school. Alex had been his typical weird self that day, making squeaky noises in back of the class, trying to convince everyone there was a mouse running loose.

Now look at him, thought Jason. He had probably gone chasing after a lost pet, too — and suffered the consequences.

Jason stooped down. He shook Alex's shoulders. "Alex! It's me, Jason. Alex!"

Two sentences popped into Jason's head. Something the Plutonium Boss had said. *"I need tough species, ones that I can mutate into new forms that serve my needs. The last time I tried that on a human, he fell apart."*

With horror, it dawned on Jason that Alex might have been that human.

"Rammmnnnf."

It was Alex's voice. He was struggling to say something.

Jason leaned close in. "What, Alex? What did you say?"

Alex's eyes flickered open, shut, then open. He fixed a steady gaze at Jason. "I said, 'Rammmnnnf,'" he replied, stone faced. "What's the matter, don't you say 'rammmnnnf' when you wake up after being knocked unconscious?"

Jason let out a howl of joy. It was Alex, all right — unmutated, with that same sick sense of humor.

"Ughh," Alex moaned, sitting up. "I dreamed I had left this place . . . or maybe that was reality and this is a dream. And if it is, what are you doing cluttering up my dream?"

"This isn't a dream, Alex," Jason said. "We're in some bizarre underworld created by the Plutonium Boss."

Alex slapped his helmet. "Oh, right, right! Of course. I'm looking for my pet lizard, while he's plotting to turn the Earth into a big charcoal briquet!"

"You remember!"

"Now I *know* I'm dreaming." Alex sank to the ground again. "Wake me up when it's over."

Jason pulled him to his feet. "You have to come with me, Alex. We both got this far; together we can beat the Plutonium Boss."

"Where's what's-her-name?" Alex asked. "The girl with the great car who dumped me."

"Eve dumped you?" Jason said. He couldn't believe it.

"Sort of, yeah. I fell down this hole and she came at me with a gun. Scared me to death. Then she said she's from another planet, told me this wacko story about the Plutonium Boss — which I didn't believe, but I thought, hey, if I play along with it she'll let me ride in the car. Then we went through some long tunnel, which I thought was never going to end. I got really nervous. Soon as we got through, she insisted I get out and go through some door. No way, Jose, I thought. I got out and ran away. Next thing I know, I was taken away by some big metal bird, and then ..." His voice trailed off.

"Then what?" Jason asked.

Alex shrugged. "I don't remember. It's all a blur, until I woke up and saw you."

"Well, the important thing is that you're alive," Jason said. "Now let's go try to find Eve. She's in trouble." He turned to run, but Alex pulled him back.

"What are you, crazy? What did she do to help me? Hey, I don't know about you, but I want to get out of here. I just got this new video game at home, and I'm finally —"

Jason cut him off. "This is more important than video games, Alex. If we don't get this Plutonium Boss, you won't ever need to worry about video games again. There won't be a world left to play them in! Now come on!"

Grumbling, Alex followed him. Together they went to SOPHIA 3rd and climbed in.

They found Level 5. While Jason slew the Underboss there, a lobster, Alex hid in a corner.

At Level 6, Alex finally began to pull himself together and helped Jason destroy that Underboss.

Driving through the tunnel to Level 7, Jason could barely control his excitement. Butterflies crashed around in his stomach, his fingers tingled with anticipation. One more Underboss, then they would come face-to-face with the most dreaded enemy the world had ever known. Just hours ago it had seemed impossible. But it was going to happen, Jason knew it.

"Are we there yet?" Alex whined.

As SOPHIA 3rd approached the end of the tunnel, Jason gave him a sidelong glance. "You know, Bufoni, you can really spoil a moment."

"Hey, ease up. I was just kid —"

The word caught in Alex's throat. SOPHIA 3rd had just shot out the tunnel and into Level 7 — and it was unlike anything they had seen.

This was no shiny metal sewer, no mud-clotted cavern. It was as if they had taken a sudden detour to the North Pole. A frigid coating of white covered every square inch. Icicles hung from the ledges that protruded from walls of solid ice. On each ledge, each pathway, there was a crusty covering of snow.

"Wow," Alex said, looking around with wonder. "The only thing missing is Rudolph the Red-Nosed Reindeer."

There were some armadillolike robots crawling around, which Jason recognized from other levels. Even though they could pelt SOPHIA 3rd with ammunition, Jason considered them easy pickings. With Alex's help, he blew them away. In front of them, a long white road stretched out.

Alex sat back in his seat. "Wake me up when we get to the end of this road."

Before he could close his eyes, Jason brought the vehicle to a screeching, skidding halt.

Alex bolted upright in his seat.

In front of them, like a winter sprite emerging from a blizzard, Eve was running toward them. She was waving energetically, and through her helmet Jason could see a smile of relief on her face.

"She's all right," Jason said, not quite believing it. Then, as she got closer, he shouted with happiness: "She's all right!"

He looked over at Alex, expecting to share a scream of triumph, a smile of recognition, *something*.

But Alex's eyes were fixed grimly forward. And his finger was on the GUN button.

Jason panicked. "Are you crazy?"

Alex didn't answer. He seemed to be taking aim.

"This is a joke, right?" Jason said. "Look, I know you were a little ticked off at her, but this really isn't funny —"

Jason reached over to push Alex's hand away.

But it wasn't a joke.

And Alex was quick — and determined. With a firm press on the button, he sent a straight line of gunfire toward Eve.

GAME HINT

You must defeat each Underboss in order to advance.

CHAPTER 17

With a bright blare of smoke, Eve went up in a miniature mushroom cloud.

SOPHIA 3rd recoiled with the impact, sliding along the ice.

Jason's mouth locked in the open position. He stared, unable to find words to describe the horror he felt.

"Well?" Alex said.

Jason's eyes slowly traveled from the mushroom cloud to Alex. His mind was an overloaded jumble of pain, rage, shock, sadness. All of which canceled each other out and became numbness.

Alex rolled his eyes. "Aren't you going to drive?"

"Aren't . . . you going to . . . drive. . . ?" Jason repeated, as if he'd forgotten how to speak. Then, suddenly, the words poured out in a torrent: "How can you ask me that? How can you be so calm, you . . . you *murderer!* She was the only survivor of her planet! She's the one who told us about the

Plutonium Boss! Without her, there would be no chance for survival. And now you've gone and ... and ..."

Tears welled up in Jason's eyes. He couldn't continue.

"Hey ... hey, easy!" Alex said. "You don't get it."

"What do you mean *I don't get it?*" Jason was practically spitting his words now.

"I mean that wasn't Eve, Jason!"

"Don't play games with me. The Plutonium Boss did mutate you, didn't he? He turned you into a ruthless killing machine."

Alex grabbed Jason by the shoulders and shook him. "Earth to Jason! Earth to Jason! Read my lips! *That wasn't Eve.*"

Jason just stared at him, his rage turning to confusion.

"The minute I saw her, something came back to me," Alex continued. "I remembered something from that time I thought I forgot." He knitted his brows, reaching into the recent past. "The Plutonium Boss ... I met him — or at least I think I did, although I can't picture how he looked. He brought me into some sort of genetics lab. He wanted to do an experiment with me or something."

"A mutation experiment," Jason said.

"Like what he did to make those Underbosses."

"I — I guess," Alex said. "Anyway, he kept complaining about me. He said I was too weak-hearted, I couldn't keep conscious — which must have been right, because I barely remember it. But there was something else going on in the lab, some new kind of imaging."

"Huh?"

"He was using nuclear magnetic resonance imaging — something like that. If he needed to hide something, he could project a moving image over it, using the nuclear magnetic rays. It looked real, but you could tell it wasn't. Something about the color, the way it glowed."

"You mean Eve was —" Jason said. "Why didn't he just use a hologram?"

"Holograms are okay for close up," Alex said, "but from a distance you can see through them. What we were seeing was a small nuclear bomb disguised with an image of Eve."

"So how come you could see her and I couldn't?"

Alex shrugged. "I guess I've been down here so long my eyesight has been, you know, *sensitized* to radioactivity or something."

"Amazing, Bufoni," Jason said with a smile. "You saved our lives."

"Hey, I'm not as stupid as I look."

Just then SOPHIA 3rd was thrown backward by a cannon blast. Jason and Alex had to get back to work. They blasted their way forward, destroying sinister ice monsters and self-propelled gun turrets.

Alex was having the time of his life. "Hey, this isn't so bad after all," he shouted, picking off an ice monster with ease. "I wouldn't mind staying here awhile."

As SOPHIA 3rd approached a sudden drop-off, Jason jammed on the brakes. "Don't speak so soon," he warned.

The vehicle went into a skid — right over the edge. Jason and Alex were both thrown to the left as SOPHIA 3rd slid down a long, icy spiral. They picked up speed, until all they could see was a white blur.

"Stop us!" Alex screamed.

Jason tried the brakes but there was no traction. He pressed EMERGENCY JUMP, but the vehicle just banged against the tunnel's ceiling.

SOPHIA 3rd barreled downward — and slid to a stop at the bottom. Only their shoulder harnesses kept Jason and Alex from flying through the windshield.

Jason exhaled with relief. He looked

out at their surroundings—a small chamber with ice-block walls. In the center of it, covered with frost, was an arched double door.

"I want to go home—*now!*" Alex demanded. "I've had enough of this!"

Jason grabbed his door handle. "Come on, Alex. I have a feeling we ain't seen nothing yet."

Reluctantly, Alex followed him to the double door. There was a huge metal ring on each half of the door, and above each ring a sign said NO TRESPASSING.

"Maybe we should knock first," Alex suggested meekly.

Jason grabbed one of the rings and pulled the door open.

A blast of frigid air greeted them, with a loud *whoooosh*. Jason and Alex were both knocked off their feet.

"I wish they'd turn down the air-conditioning," Alex said with a weak smile.

They picked themselves up, and Jason led the way in. Howling winds swirled above them. They looked up. Blades of ice jutted out of the walls, forming crystal caves and catacombs. Shadows danced and flitted, like bats. Aside from the wind and bizarre squeaky noises, there was silence.

"Come on, Jason," Alex pleaded.

"There's nothing here. This is probably not even the Plutonium Boss's jurisdiction."

R-beeeeeeeeeeeeeak!

The noise startled both of them. They looked around and saw nothing.

"I know that noise," Jason said quietly.

R-beeeeeeeeeeeeeeak!

Now there was a knocking sound. From behind the wall to their right.

From behind a door in the wall.

"This can't be," Jason murmured.

"What? What?" Alex said. "You're getting weird on me all of a sudden."

R-beeeeeeeeeeeeeak!

"This is just like ... like my dream," Jason answered.

He approached the door. The icy, slimy knob was there, just as in the dream. He was gripped with fear. He didn't want to face what was in there — *couldn't* face it. No robot, no monster, no Underboss, *nothing* compared to the horror of this creature.

But in his dream he never did see the creature — or did he? The end of the dream had been so terrifying that Jason had awakened rather than face it.

This time, when Jason opened the door, he would be wide awake. There was no escaping.

He grabbed the knob, felt the icy stuff oozing between his fingers. With a mighty pull, he yanked it open.

Pitch-black. Inky black. Black-hole black.

Nothing. Just like the dream.

"L-l-let's get out of here," Alex whimpered.

For a moment, Jason agreed. But only a moment. He stepped forward, looking up into the suffocating darkness. When he spoke, he said three well-chosen words:

"Come get me."

R-beeeeeeeeeeeeeak!

The shriek almost pierced his eardrums. Alex yelled in pain. A blinding burst of light shattered the blackness.

And there before them stood the last Underboss.

Jason drew his gun, then dropped it.

He fell to his knees. "No...no. I can't."

The Underboss came nearer. It loomed over them, its tongue lashing in and out of its mouth.

"Kill it, Jason!" Alex shrieked.

But Jason just bowed his head. He could vanquish robots without a second thought. He could turn Underbosses to dust. Nothing would make him happier than destroying the Plutonium Boss, if he had the chance.

But he couldn't — just couldn't — raise his gun against his own frog.

The seventh and last Underboss was Fred.

GAME HINT

Use curved bullets to
kill the bullet machine
on Level 2.

CHAPTER 18

"What is happening to you?" Alex's voice was getting closer. "Give *me* the laser!"

Jason spun around and grabbed the gun. "Don't you touch him!" he said through clenched teeth.

Alex stared at him, dumbfounded. "Jason, he is a monster! He is going to kill us! Do you want to die? I hope not, because I will be really angry if you leave me alone down here."

A long, fiery tongue whipped out of the creature's mouth. It brushed against both Jason and Alex, flinging them across the room like paper dolls.

"Agggghhhhh!" Alex cried out, tumbling head over heels. He landed next to a ten-foot-high granite boulder. Wincing with pain, he looked up at Jason. "*Now* are you happy? Gee, it sure is fun getting knocked against a humongous rock. Maybe next time he'll throw us *through* it."

The creature was eyeing them from across the room. It squatted on its hind legs, then sprang into the air.

Its shadow enveloped the white floor in black. Jason and Alex looked up helplessly as the mammoth amphibian plummeted back toward them.

Alex grabbed Jason's arm. "Come on!"

He pulled Jason behind the boulder. They fell to the floor. When the frog landed, the room shook as if it had exploded.

"Now, would you mind coming to your senses?" Alex demanded. "Or at least give me your gun so I can blast that ugly thing to pieces!"

Jason looked up at Alex. His eyes were rimmed with red. The fierceness in his face had melted away. All that was left was a shattered and lonely boy. "Alex," he said, his voice cracking, "that ugly thing is my pet frog."

Alex backed off. He stared at Jason for a second or two, processing the last statement. Then, measuring his words carefully, he said, "Jason Frudnick, you have truly gone whacko. Maybe you ought to stay here and cool out for a second, while I —"

"I'm serious, Alex!"

"Sure, Jason. You kept him in your garage, right? A special garage, four stories high — with padding on the ceiling to cushion his head when he jumps!"

Jason grabbed Alex's shoulders. "Listen to me, will you? You know the kind of stuff the Plutonium Boss is into — genetic engineering, nuclear mutations. He turned my little pet frog into that . . . that thing."

R-beeeeeeeeeeeeeeak!

There was a loud cracking noise on the other side of the rock. Fred was trying to knock a path around the edge.

"How can you be sure it's him?" Alex asked.

"I just know. When you've been with a pet every day of his life, you get to know him like a person. If Fred were in a room with all the other frogs on Long Island, I would be able to tell him apart in a second."

Alex nodded. "Yeah. I felt the same way about Plutarch."

"Plutarch?"

"My pet lobster." Alex lowered his eyes. "He was the fifth Underboss."

"So you knew I wasn't crazy all along!" Jason said. "Why didn't you say anything when we were in Level Five?"

R-beeeeeeeeeeeeeeak!

The rock shook. Fragments of granite shot upward, from the other side of the rock. If Fred couldn't get around, he was going to blast his way though.

"I didn't say anything, Jason, because it really *wasn't* Plutarch."

"But you just said —"

"This is my point, Jason. Our pets are gone. The minute the Plutonium Boss began changing them, they became something different. Robots. Killing machines. Whatever personalities they had are history, pal. Just remember, you are no longer looking at Fred. You are facing a creation of the most evil creature the world has known. We've destroyed all his Underbosses, and now he's trying to prey on our weaknesses. He knows we'd never fire at our own pets. But he's wrong, Jason — because Fred and Plutarch are dead. He killed them. And you know what? If they could, they would be cheering us on right now."

R-beeeeeeeeeeeeeak!

The entire top of the boulder flew off, crashing into the wall to their left.

They dove to the ground for cover. Jason reached for his gun. When he sat up, his face was set with grim determination. "You know, Bufoni, I never thought I would hear you say something that made sense."

Alex smiled. "We're in this together?"

"Let's go," was Jason's reply. Holding the laser with two hands, he stepped around the boulder. He planted his feet in firing position.

The creature that was once Fred turned to face him. His mouth was twisted into a horrible leer. Smoke billowed out from between its lips.

Before it had the chance to shoot out its tongue, Jason opened fire.

R-beeeeeeeeeeeeeak!
R-beeeeeeeeeeeeeak!

The scream sliced through Jason, from his head to his toes, by way of his heart. The force of the explosion threw him backward. The light was as intense as five suns. Ice and dirt began falling from the ceiling.

Huddled on the ground, he thought about time travel — going back, taking back the shot. If only he could . . .

When he looked up, he caught a last glimpse of Fred — more gas than solid, vaporizing before his eyes. On Fred's face was an expression — clear as day. It was a look of shock, fear, betrayal. The same look Jason had seen when Fred had disappeared into the swamp. His head turned toward Jason, and he let out a tiny, helpless *ribit*.

The next moment, Fred was gone.

CHAPTER 19

"No." Jason's voice was raw with emotion. Then, with the force of a megaton blast, he understood what he had just done. A scream welled up from the bottom of his gut. "NOOOOOOOOOOO!"

A falling chunk of ice just missed his head. "Come on, let's get out of here!" he heard Alex shout.

Jason wheeled around. "You . . . lied to me," he said. "That was Fred — or at least there was some of him left. Some hope. But now — now he's —"

More ice and soil spat toward them as a wall suddenly collapsed.

Alex grabbed Jason by the wrist. "Later for that! This place is caving in!"

Jason realized his friend was right. Fred was gone, but now they had to save their own lives.

They ran out the door and into the outer room. There, blades of ice were raining from the roof like oversized sleet.

"What a way to go!" Alex shouted. "Impaled on an icicle!"

It was getting harder to maneuver. The ground was covered with piles of debris. Jason fell, then Alex. The outer door was now twenty feet away.

Alex moaned. "My ankle —"

Jason pulled him up. He put an arm around his friend's shoulder. "Here, lean on me." Together, they began hobbling to the door.

But it was too late. A refrigerator-sized chunk of the ceiling fell in front of the door.

"Great," Alex said. "What now?"

Jason opened his mouth to answer, but he was interrupted.

"What now? Do you think you have a choice?"

The force of the Plutonium Boss's voice alone was like a dynamite blast. Jason and Alex were flattened against the floor.

There wasn't time to think. Then, Jason and Alex were lifted off the floor. They hovered in the air, as if supported by invisible hands.

"What the —" was all Alex could say before he and Jason began to move.

Through the air. Through walls. Through tunnels. At blinding speed.

They passed through every level, every room. All the robots, all the enemies they had faced now stood motionless, silently

94

watching Jason and Alex speed by. They shot toward granite walls, steel walls. Each time, they covered their heads — but when they passed through, they didn't feel a thing. Somehow, they were being protected. They were travelling in another dimension. They were being saved for . . . *something*.

And when they stopped, they had an idea what that something was.

Standing before them was the Plutonium Boss.

GAME HINT

After you defeat the Underboss in Level 6, get the wall walking power, go back to Level 2, and find the secret door for Level 7.

CHAPTER 20

"Welcome, my human friends. You are made of tougher stuff than I expected."

Up close, the voice was unbearable. Jason covered his ears and dropped to his knees.

He couldn't look. Part of it was the brightness — so intense that it seemed to burn through his eyes. But mainly Jason was shielding himself from the very *appearance* of the Plutonium Boss.

The first Underboss had been a hideous, boiling mass of nuclear matter. The others had been horrible mutations of pet animals.

But they were nothing — in fact, compared to the Plutonium Boss, they were almost *beautiful*.

Through slitted eyes, Jason forced himself to look at his nemesis, at the monster who had destroyed his beloved Fred.

First, there was the head. A head the size of a building. Two huge muscle lumps were where the eyes should have been. Fleshy folds rippled down the center of the head, ending in a gruesome mouth surrounded by horns. The mouth was in constant motion, dripping fireballs, revealing jagged, daggerlike teeth. Its chin tapped the ground, sending out sparks.

The head had no body. Instead, two muscular legs jutted out from each side. They curved outward, then hooked downward to the ground. At the knee joints, sharp spikes glistened. Gnarled feet clutched the ground with wide, sharp claws.

"What's the matter?" the Plutonium Boss taunted, fire spitting from its mouth. **"You do not find me attractive?"**

"Get it away from me!" Alex said. "I hate rats!"

Jason looked at his friend. "Rats? Where do you see —"

"Silence!" the Plutonium Boss cut him off. **"I must admit, I underestimated you humans. You have proven to be much, much stronger than expected. What you did was a feat of courage and cunning. Perhaps you are now afraid that your journey is in vain, that I will simply vanquish you right now. But you are wrong. I intend to reward you."**

Jason and Alex exchanged an uneasy glance.

"For this Lonor, I have chosen only one other person." Rocking from foot to foot, the Plutonium Boss stepped aside.

Jason and Alex both froze. Neither of them had paid attention to what was behind the Plutonium Boss. Now they saw. It was a white, curved wall, stretching out and away from them on both sides for what looked like miles. In the center of it was a giant metal door covered with gauges, switches, and pipes.

Chained to one of the pipes, looking haggard and exhausted, was Eve.

"Jason!" she said, her voice hoarse. "He is a rat — to Alex. To me, he's a horrible flying predator from Signar-el. To you, he's something else. The Plutonium Boss actually has no form visible to the naked eye. He takes the shape of something that he knows will frighten you — for each person, the form is different."

Jason didn't know what to say. Was she real? She had to be. The Plutonium Boss had no need to fake him out anymore.

He turned to the Boss and drew his gun. "You rotten coward."

"Jason, no!" Alex shouted. "He'll kill us all!"

Jason ignored his friend. He fired.

The Plutonium Boss took the full force of the laser blast. Nothing happened. There was no color change, no scream of pain. He simply opened his mouth.

Out flew a brilliant flare of light. It shot directly toward Jason's hand. The gun went flying away, and clattered on the floor.

"Yeeeeaah!" Jason looked down at his hand. It was untouched, except for a slight black mark where the gun had been.

The Plutonium Boss's laugh once again assaulted his senses. **"A peculiar way to show gratitude — especially after I have deemed you worthy to test my new creation."**

"Wh-what are you t-talking about?" Alex stammered.

"The structure before you is my cyclotron. With it, I will be able to accelerate my plans for the Earth. No more waiting around for eons, like I did at Signar-el. I will be able to create enough atomic energy to wipe out the planet immediately!" He roared with self-satisfaction. **"However, in my haste to build it, I have not been able to test it adequately. I need a few... volunteers — say, three."**

"Count me out!" Alex snapped. "Just point me to the nearest blowhole, and I'm out of here!"

Suddenly Alex began moving toward the cyclotron. Not walking, not running. His feet were dragging on the ground, as if he were being pulled. "Hey!" Alex's upper body struggled to throw itself in the opposite direction. "Hey, what's going on?"

Jason looked down. The same thing was happening to him. His eyes widened with terror as the cyclotron loomed closer.

Suddenly some of the switches on the door started to move by themselves. A whirring noise began. A red neon sign flashed CYCLE BEGINNING.

The dull green glow around them diminished. Even the Plutonium Boss seemed to become a duller, lighter color.

The cyclotron was sapping the energy of the entire underworld. The radiation from the walls, the power of the robots — all of it was being drawn to the white machine before them. All of it was collecting inside the door.

"Nooooo!" Jason and Alex shouted as they were drawn closer.

But there was no defense. In seconds, they would be ripped apart without a trace.

CHAPTER 21

"Jason, look!" Eve screamed, clinging to the pipe for dear life. "Look at the Boss! He's using his reserves of nuclear power to start up the cyclotron!"

"Of course!" Alex yelled. "What else can he use? There are no electrical outlets down here!"

"But he needs that power for himself, too!" Eve answered. "He's nothing without it! Look at him!"

Jason glanced over his shoulder. In the room's dim light, the Plutonium Boss seemed to be flickering. For a split second, he glowed brightly, then sputtered.

Jason looked downward. Despite the diminished power, he was still being dragged along. Not as strongly as before, but strongly enough to prevent his escape. Out of the corner of his eye, he saw his laser gun on the ground. It was only about five feet away. If he could only tear free of the Boss's hold . . .

With his every last ounce of strength,

101

he threw himself toward the gun.

There was a *dzzzit* sound, a breaking of some sort of force field. Jason hurtled through the air. He landed inches from the gun.

Instantly, he was jerked back up again. The invisible field was pulling him with double the force.

But his fingers were now wrapped around his laser gun.

"You are wasting your energy!" the Plutonium Boss called out, his voice half the volume it once was. **"Those bullets have no effect on me!"**

"Maybe not on you, dinosaur face," Jason said. He swung the gun around toward the cyclotron wall, pointing it at a spot near the Boss. "But it looks like your great invention is made of earth materials." He took careful aim.

Beeoo-beeoo-beeoo! A large hole ripped open in the cyclotron wall.

The Plutonium Boss fell to the ground with a resounding *foooom*. He began sliding toward the hole. The cyclotron's energy was pulling him in.

"Grrrrrrraaaaaaaaaaaaagghhh!" His scream made Jason's skin tingle.

Jason, Alex, and Eve all fell limply. Eve's chains had vanished. They were free.

"He's using all his own energy to save himself," Eve said. "Let's run!"

A sudden explosion tore up the ground, inches from their faces. They spun around.

"**Die, you insects!**" the Plutonium Boss shrieked. Three pulsating energy orbs shot out of his mouth.

Pooooosh!
Pooooosh!
Pooooosh!

Jason, Alex, and Eve dove away. Scrambling to his feet, Jason pointed his gun at the Boss.

His shots hit their mark. This time, the Boss let out a cry of pain.

The cyclotron's power was picking up. The Boss flailed his legs helplessly. Green and yellow sparks discharged from the pores of his skin. As he slid toward the hole, he left a trail of glowing purple slime.

"**You . . . cannot . . . escape!**" the Boss said.

Three more energy orbs burst out of his mouth. Jason shot at them, deflecting them in midair.

The Boss was now at the hole. He swung his legs around. He braced them on either side. The suction of the cyclotron pulled at his face-body, stretching it, making its horrible features even more grotesque. He pulled against it, letting out a furious howl.

Then, with a sickening pop, the Plutonium Boss was sucked inside.

There was no time to feel relief. The cyclotron began to rumble furiously. There was a high-pitched squeal. A sign on the door flashed MALFUNCTION! STRUCTURAL DAMAGE!

Huge chunks of stone and dirt began falling around them. "Here we go again!" Alex cried out.

"This is for real!" Jason said. "That thing is going to blow!"

"Let's get out of here!" Alex yelled, grabbing his two friends' arms.

Eve pulled him back. She looked him in the face. Sweat was pouring down her brow, making rivulets past her bloodshot eyes. "There's no place to go! Don't you see? When the cyclotron explodes, the world goes with it!"

CHAPTER 22

Sudden bursts of energy rattled the entire area. The cyclotron was chugging, wheezing, popping, shaking. The ground shifted and vibrated. Jason was seeing double. His stomach was turning.

There was one thought in his mind. One thought only. *We set out to save the world, and now we're destroying it.*

Struggling to keep his balance, he walked toward the cyclotron.

"What are you doing?" Eve shouted.

"Shutting it off!" Jason replied.

"How?" Alex said.

"I don't know!" Jason was at the door now. He grabbed a lever and pulled. A wild pinging noise began, making the machine shake even more.

The next instant, Alex was by his side. "You're making it worse!" he shouted. Alex began yanking levers and pressing buttons, left and right.

Eve joined them. Together they frantically punched, jabbed, turned.

The machine churned even more violently. It sparked and spewed gases.

Then, an explosion ripped another hole in its side.

All three of them were blown backward. They landed in a heap, fifteen feet from the machine. The sign on the door flashed OVERLOAD! OVERLOAD! OVERLOAD!

Jason braced himself for the end of the world.

CHAPTER 23

When he opened his eyes, he saw Alex and Eve hunched on the ground. They were covering their heads, waiting.

The air was filled with flying debris and thick smoke. Piles of rocks and metal littered the ground.

But something was different.

Through the smoke, he peered at the cyclotron. The bright sign had stopped flashing.

He got up. Picking his path carefully, he walked toward it.

There was rumbling, but it was distant. It wasn't coming from the cyclotron — or was it?

He was a few feet away from the door now. He brushed away the smoke with his hands.

The gauges all rested at zero. The lights were out, the beeps were silent.

The cyclotron was dead.

He turned around and yelled at the top of his lungs: "We did it!"

He ran back to Alex and Eve. Both of them were straining to see him. "We made the cyclotron burn itself out!" Jason said. "It's off — kaput!"

There was silence for a moment. Silence that was followed by the loud *crrack* of a collapsing wall. Mud gushed out toward them.

"And so are we!" Alex said.

Eve grabbed them both. "Follow me!"

The three of them ran, making their way through the surrounding chaos. Eve took them through smoke-filled tunnels, doors that had been blown apart. At the end of one corridor, a metal door remained tightly shut. "SOPHIA 3rd is in here," she said.

Alex shook his head. "No. Jason and I left it —"

"It's in here!" Eve insisted. "The Plutonium Boss was a loudmouth — he told me all his little secrets, like his plans to turn SOPHIA 3rd into his own underground pleasure vehicle. When he brought you to the cyclotron, this room is where he brought SOPHIA 3rd."

"Step back," Jason said. The others obeyed, and he blasted the door open.

Sure enough, SOPHIA 3rd was sitting there, waiting.

With a solid chunk of granite on his

hood. A solid chunk of granite that had smashed its engine.

Jason's heart sank. But Eve just ran up to the hood. "Help me," she said. "There's an auxiliary rear engine, but we'll go faster without this thing!"

With every ounce of strength, the three of them managed to push the rock off. They jumped inside, and Eve started the spare engine.

It let out only a meager whine, but it worked. Eve steered out of the room.

"Do you know how to get out?" Alex asked.

"Up," Eve said. "Other than that, beats me!"

They zoomed through a jagged hole in a nearby wall. They emerged into a cavern Jason recognized. It was Level 4. Concentrating on every detail, they were able to retrace their steps.

Level 3 was empty. Mud poured through holes in the walls and short-circuited robots were flailing on the ground.

Level 2 was unrecognizable. Twisted remains of the metal walls lay on the ground like shipwrecks.

Level 1 was by now a churning pit of lava and slime.

They raced through the final tunnel

and into the chamber where Jason had first met Eve. At one end, Jason could see the bottom of the blowhole chute.

"Let's see if we still have some of that weapon power," Eve said. She reached over and pressed HOVER GAUGE.

SOPHIA 3rd left the ground. It shot into the chute and slowly rose upward through the blowhole.

Around them, the side of the hole trembled. Jason looked up. There was daylight. It was far away, but it was there. Behind them, the blowhole was caving in. Its walls were bursting, spewing soil and rocks.

Eve kept her finger on the hover gauge, but SOPHIA 3rd was slowing down. "I don't know if we're going to make it!" she cried out.

"I can see the surface!" Jason replied. "Just hang on for a little while longer — please!"

"I don't have any control over it!" Eve shot back.

And she was right. With a sputter and a groan, the hover power died. In fact, the entire vehicle died.

They seemed to stand still for a moment, and then they plunged toward the pandemonium below.

CHAPTER 24

Thunk.

SOPHIA 3rd had stopped. It wasn't until then that Jason realized his eyes were slammed shut and his teeth were clenched.

He unshut and unclenched.

"What the —"

They were on solid ground. Solid ground that had filled in the blowhole. Above them, sunlight streamed in through the opening in the swamp.

"Doesn't do us any good to sit here," Alex said. "Let's go!"

The three of them left the vehicle. The sides of the hole were sloped toward the top. They were sticky with moist earth and clots of grass. Perfect footholds.

In minutes they reached the surface. Jason took a deep breath. The midday sun blazed down, releasing gases from stagnant pools of water. In the heavy humidity, mosquitoes buzzed around, happy to find three victims. At this time of the year, the swamp was at its worst level of odor and infestation.

To Jason, it was beautiful. "We made it," he said, half-believing it wasn't true.

Alex sighed and looked at the ground. Below him, the thundering underworld was rumbling. Jason knew what was on Alex's mind — Fred and Plutarch. Sure, the three of them had made it, and yes, it looked like the world would never know the horror of the Plutonium Boss.

But it came at a price. Small as it may have been, it would always hurt. Life would never be the same without the two pets they had tried in vain to save.

Eve took a sniff left, then right. Her face curled into a sneer. "*This* is the atmosphere you breathe?"

Jason held back a smile. "Yes, is something wrong?"

"It is rich in — "

"Stink factor," Alex said with a straight face.

"Yes, quite stinked," Eve replied, her nose still twitching. "I do not know if I could get used to it."

Jason couldn't hold it any longer. He burst into giggles, rolling on the swamp floor. In an instant he was covered with mud. But he didn't mind. He was home, stinked or not.

With a smile on his face, he stretched out right then and there, and fell fast asleep.

> ### GAME HINT
>
> To defeat Underbosses on levels 2,4,6, and 7, try this technique: Use the A button to fire grenades as quickly as possible. When the Under-boss starts flashing white, hit the PAUSE button, wait about 30 seconds, then resume. You'll discover that he's dead.

CHAPTER 25

"...*federal officials expressed surprise at the magnitude of yesterday's quake. There is a minor fault line approximately under Batrachia, they say, but the chance of feeling a tremor is about one in thirteen million.*"

The sound of the kitchen radio drifted into Jason's room the next morning, waking him up. As he did every Sunday morning, he thrust the pillow over his head and tried to go back to sleep. And as he did every Sunday morning, he realized it wasn't going to work. It was time to get up.

But when his eyes popped open, a flood of images popped into his head. SOPHIA 3rd...Eve...Alex...voices...robots... horrible laughter.

Jason sat bolt upright. It was a dream, wasn't it? It had to be. He was filled with happiness and relief. Imagine thinking he had plunged underground and chased after a plutonium mutant. Imagine thinking he had actually lost Fred.

Fred!

He hopped out of bed and ran to Fred's habitat.

When his head began to pound like John Henry's hammer, he knew something had happened.

When he looked into Fred's home, he knew he hadn't been dreaming. It was empty.

Letting out a deep sigh, he sank back into bed. He was barely aware when his parents called up to say they were going shopping.

He was barely aware of the doorbell ringing minutes later. Or was it hours later? Jason didn't know and didn't care.

But it rang a second time, and a third. Each ring pulsed through him like a mild electric shock. Jason was annoyed. He wanted to tell whoever it was to leave him alone. He stood up and shuffled downstairs.

Briiing!

Jason wished his parents had gotten a doorbell that didn't sound like the bell that rang between classes. He clutched the doorknob and pulled it open.

R-beeeeeeeeeeeeeak!

He jumped clear off the ground. It was a frog — as tall as he was, with a grimacè that turned its face into a mask of evil.

"No!" Jason shouted. He scrambled to

his feet. How could this have happened? How could this thing have escaped?

He was numb with terror. Without thinking, he slammed the door shut.

"Yeoooow!" came a muffled voice from the other side. "Hey, come on! Is that any way to treat a friend?"

Jason stared blankly at the door. He knew that voice. Confused, he opened it again.

"Alex?" he said.

The latex frog head hung limp in Alex's right hand. Alex scratched his head, which was peeking out of a green frog costume. Behind him, Eve was rolling on the front lawn with laughter.

"I was going to say 'trick or treat,'" Alex said. "But I guess you already decided against the treat."

"Sorry!" Jason said. "I thought you were —"

"I know," Alex replied. "You thought I was Underboss Number Seven, your mutated pet frog. You mean to tell me, you'd slam the door if your own pet came to it?"

"Well, no, of course not. But —"

"Then how come you did?"

Jason fell silent. He stared at Alex, befuddled. "But ... I didn't. It was *you*. Are you being weird again?"

Ribit.

Jason felt a pang. The noise sounded so much like Fred, he could feel his heart breaking. "That was . . . a good imitation, Alex. But I wish you wouldn't —"

Ribit.

Alex shook his head. "Couldn't do it if I tried. How about looking down, buddy? You won't make eye contact up there."

Jason lowered his eyes. When his gaze reached the front mat, it stayed there. He felt his blood pounding through his veins. He felt his vision get blurry, then sharp again.

Sharp enough to see that Fred was at his feet. Sharp enough to see a little hint of a frog smile on his face.

He kneeled down. He picked the frog up in his hand. "It is you, isn't it?"

Ribit, came the answer.

Jason felt his eyes start to water — until Alex let out a loud groan. "Oh, please! I thought the soaps didn't start for a couple of hours!"

It was then that Jason noticed the lobster crawling on the lawn behind Alex. "Plutarch?" Jason asked.

"In the flesh!" Alex answered.

"What — how —"

"Hey, don't knock it," Alex said. "Why ask questions?"

Eve stepped up to Jason's doorstep. "I

believe I know," she said. "Remember the first Underboss? It was nothing but a pure nuclear creation. Well, I think they were all like that, really. But the Plutonium Boss thought he could scare you by covering them with grotesque images of familiar objects."

"Like Fred and Plutarch," Jason said.

"Exactly."

"But how could they have possibly escaped?"

"You underestimate the power of a pet to follow its master," Eve replied. "My theory is that they were being held somewhere close to us. When we escaped, they found a way to chase after us."

"And we were so frantic we didn't see them stowing away!" Alex added.

Ribit.

"Fred agrees," Jason said with a smile. He looked at Alex, then at Eve. Suddenly his face got serious. "What about you, Eve? Where will you go now?"

"I have told Alex's parents about my past," Eve said.

Jason was shocked. "What?"

"They love that kind of stuff!" Alex said. "We'll tell everybody that Eve is a distant cousin who's been orphaned, and Mom and Dad had to take her in. Eve promised to tell them all kinds of outer space stories."

"And in return, they promised they would never spill the prunes about me."

Ribit.

"Fred says, 'beans,' Eve. Uh, I have a feeling you better stay away from the 'sling' for a while."

Alex tried to hold back a giggle, but it was hopeless. Jason joined him, and then Eve.

And as Fred and Plutarch stared in confusion, their masters shared their first good laugh together.

The first of many.

Dear Reader,

I hope you liked reading *Blaster Master*. Here is a list of some other books that I thought you might like:

A Journey to the Center of the Earth
by Jules Verne

My Teacher Is an Alien
by Bruce Coville

Starship Troopers
by Robert Heinlein

The War of the Worlds
by H.G. Wells

The White Mountains (trilogy)
by John Christopher

A Wrinkle in Time
by Madeleine L'Engle

You can find these books at your local library or bookstore. Ask your teacher or librarian for other books you might enjoy.

Best wishes,

F.X. Nine

Enter the
WORLDS OF POWER™
GIVEAWAY!

WIN A NINTENDO® GAME BOY™ COMPACT VIDEO GAME SYSTEM!

You'll *score big* if your entry is picked in this awesome drawing! Just look what you could win:

GRAND PRIZE:

10 Grand Prize winners!

A Nintendo® GAME BOY™ compact video game system

SECOND PRIZE:

A cool video game carrying case

25 Second Prize winners!

Rules: Entries must be postmarked by November 5, 1990. Winners will be picked at random and notified by mail. No purchase necessary. Void where prohibited. Taxes on prizes are the responsibility of the winners and their immediate families. Employees of Scholastic Inc; its agencies, affiliates, subsidiaries; and their immediate families not eligible. For a complete list of winners, send a self-addressed, stamped envelope to Worlds of Power Giveaway, Contest Winners List, at the address provided below.

Fill in the coupon below or write the information on a 3" x 5" piece of paper and mail to: **WORLDS OF POWER GIVEAWAY**, Scholastic Inc., P.O. Box 742, 730 Broadway, New York, NY 10003. Entries must be postmarked by November 5, 1990. (Canadian residents, mail entries to: Iris Ferguson, Scholastic Inc., 123 Newkirk Road, Richmond Hill, Ontario, Canada L4C365.)

Nintendo® is a registered trademark of Nintendo of America Inc. Game Boy™ is a trademark of Nintendo of America Inc. **WORLDS OF POWER** ™ Books are not authorized, sponsored or endorsed by Nintendo of America.

Worlds of Power Giveaway

Name_____ Age_____

Street_____

City_____ State_____ Zip_____

Where did you buy this <u>Worlds of Power</u> book?

❏ Bookstore ❏ Video Store ❏ Discount Store ❏ Book Club

❏ Book Fair ❏ Other_____(specify)

WOP190